# LOVE CATCH'N COWBOY

Billionaire Cowboys of Lone Star, Texas,
Book Three

# HOPE MOORE

# Love Catch'n Cowboy

Ace Buckley lost his parents when he and his twin were ten, and were raised by their uncle and aunt with all their cousins. He's strong, determined, and a lover of both ranching *and* fishing. He's too busy for love, or the chance of finding it and leaving behind children if something ever happened to him. Basically, he's a chicken and hides it behind loving the outdoors too much to take a chance.

Kelsy Camry has come to Lone Star to be closer to the grandfather she hasn't seen in years because of family issues. Her grandfather's antique fishing store holds much joy from years gone by but it's his main customer, Ace, who holds her attention most. The strong, handsome cowboy is stirring up a herd of emotions she's not ready for…but her heart keeps floating to the surface every time he turns those amazing blue-green eyes on her.

Can love find them when they both have deep, serious reasons to evade it?

In Lone Star, Texas, the pastures are green, the water is inviting, and love…it's undeniable.

# CHAPTER ONE

Ace Buckley looked around town on Friday afternoon. He'd come into town to help the store owners get ready for the dance they'd have tomorrow night. These dances were about to become a normal thing, and the entire town was in agreement if their smiles and happy chatter was an indication.

He enjoyed watching everyone's excitement and he enjoyed dancing some too, so he wasn't complaining about the new way the town was heading, getting business by having town events for all the store owners' weekend visitors. But now he was going into Lumas Camry's New and Antique Field and Stream Supplies store. Lumas had told him this morning when he saw him that he had a lure in that Ace would want to see. And of course, if anybody knew how much Ace enjoyed fishing, it was Lumas.

That man might be older, but that didn't matter—he knew his way around when it came to fishing, and he knew that Ace was in his favorite place when he was ranching or fishing. And in the morning, he would be fishing like he was most Saturday mornings when he didn't have to check cattle first thing in the morning. That was a semi day off, although ranching wasn't a profession where you had certain days off or even a day off, unless you had someone stand in for you. This was a busy time of year but he still found time to fish. And Lumas knew it. So, as far as he knew right now, he would be fishing at sunrise in the morning.

Then, tomorrow evening, after he had helped feed cattle, he was going to, he guessed, clean up and come enjoy watching everyone in town and all the newcomers who had been invited by the store owners come to enjoy the town dance. Then again, there was his new sister-in-law Sydney—well, not really his sister-in-law; he and her husband Dustin were cousins, not brothers, but they all seemed like brothers, so he didn't really know what to call her or his other cousin West's wife, Genna. But

Sydney and Dustin had just married, and he'd helped them build a new goat pen out at Sydney's family house that was now a newly opened bed-and-breakfast—and boy, were they expecting a houseful coming into town tonight and tomorrow for the weekend.

He thought the place had like eight guest rooms and, unlike he'd be, Dustin, Sydney, and her little daughter Hazel were thrilled to have a house packed full of people. Of course, having new goats in her new pen was what really had Hazel so excited—that, and showing them off to the guests. Plus, top that off with having a new daddy, and Ace hadn't seen a happier little girl in his life. And Dustin, well, watching him fall in love had been cool. Dustin didn't mind that his new sweet wife had loved another man with all her heart, lost him and then, without even planning to look for anyone to replace the man she'd lost, she and Dustin had found each other. And now they'd started their new life.

Yeah, he'd been thinking about that more than he'd have ever thought he would. He was, of all the Buckley men—his twin and his five cousins—the baby of the family. His brother Hunter was a whole fifteen minutes older than him, but none of them let him forget that he was the baby.

He didn't care. One thing about him was he was easy. Yep, he was easy all right—he'd lost his mom and dad when he was ten, him and his brother, and he'd forced himself to handle it well. Yeah, *forced*. It hadn't been as easy as he'd tried to make everybody think, but he'd handled it. And unlike some people, he and Hunter had been blessed because they'd been taken in with open arms by their uncle and aunt and *all* of his cousins. They'd not just opened their arms, but their hearts and their home to him and Hunter here in Lone Star, Texas, on the ranch. And they'd fallen into life with everyone just as if they were brothers. And that's what it felt like…unless he let his thoughts go to the two people he missed with all of his heart.

He smiled as he thought about them. They hadn't died without making sure that they'd made the right choices on what would happen to him and Hunter if they did die. Of course, because his uncle Troy was his dad Jed's brother, that made them their closest relative; his mom Loretta had been an only child and, like them, had lost her parents early. But Uncle Troy was a great man and Aunt Christine was a wonderful woman; his parents knew this and had made sure this was where they would end up if something had happened to take them away. Being here with his family was one more thing he had to be thankful about, not sad. He had one smart mom and dad, and a wonderful aunt and uncle. And grandparents. He smiled; he had great grandparents.

He stepped onto the sidewalk and headed to the door of *New and Antique Field and Stream Supplies*. They had old and new stuff, but he loved checking out old things that men had used long ago. He had a feeling that was what Lumas had waiting for him. He was a cool man, too. He had lived here a long time, although he hadn't been here his whole life. He'd chosen this town—just like a lot of people had—moved here, opened this store, and dug in deep with what he loved with new and old fishing supplies.

Lumas never talked about his family or his past. But one thing about Lone Star: the people weren't that nosey, and if anybody knew anything about his past or his family, they didn't say anything. And he didn't care.

He liked Lumas, and sometimes felt bad for him because he lived here alone—always had. Ace knew Lumas had family somewhere, he just didn't talk about them. There was a picture in Lumas's office of a young girl, a pretty blonde of about eight, standing with him on a pier. It looked like it might be in Florida, maybe the far end at the Keys. The water was a vivid blue, and they looked happy. He was kneeling down beside her as she held a fish on a line, and someone took their picture. He knew that Lumas was younger in the picture, so whoever she was, she was probably grown up by now. He never mentioned her, never talked about anybody; he just talked about fishing. And getting people to town.

Everybody in town was talking about that these days, since the ladies had come up with a plan to thank all their customers who came from all over on weekends to shop. They were now throwing them these dances every month or so. The first one had worked out great, drawing people in and helping Dustin and Sydney to meet and fall in love. Dances were obviously good places to meet someone you might want to date. Or like him, just enjoy watching everyone have a good time.

A dance was involved when Jace Calhoun, who ran a ranch and helped his granddad out at the feed store, had reunited with his old love, and now they were married and happy. And then his cousin West and Genna, who had come up with this idea, had figured things out between them, and a dance had been involved. So lately, dances had become important to the town.

West lived on the section of the ranch where their grandparents had started out, and all the goats lived there too. The goats that his grandmother had brought into the plan when she'd married his gramps. Goats were fairly strong in the family and good matchmakers. They seemed like a draw to his cousins, and he'd helped build the pens at the B&B to hold Hazel's new goats in. Dustin had teased him since then that maybe he might be the next Buckley to fall in love. Ace had made sure he knew falling in love was not in his plan and he had his reasons. They were deep and strong, and he wasn't breaking them. He'd had his own experience with heart hurts, and he wasn't ever having a child and taking a chance on leaving it behind with the pain that it caused.

He'd seen that pain in Hazel's eyes, the pain that Dustin had been drawn to and needed to help fix with the goats. Ace smiled; it was complicated, sad, and sweet. It had been awesome to see the love and joy in Sydney's and Hazel's eyes that love had helped produce.

But it wasn't for him. Nope, he liked ranching—and fishing whenever he had the chance. And when he came to the dances, he might dance one or two dances but there was no romance involved. Nope, he went to the dances because he enjoyed watching everyone in town have fun and he liked visiting with them.

So, in the morning, he was going fishing after he walked in here and found out what Lumas had waiting for him. Then he'd play with it out at the creek tomorrow morning, experiment with it and hopefully catch a few fish. If not, he'd still have a good time.

One thing his uncle and dad had had was a huge ranch. It had lots of rivers, creeks, and lakes. They had enough places to fish that he was never going to run out of spots to reel them in. Yes, he had gone fishing a few other places. Once he'd gone down to the Florida Keys and fished offshore with a buddy. He'd had a great time.

One day, it had been rough water but great fishing; lots of others out there experienced the same thing, catching mahi-mahi, a blue and green toned fish that was great to eat and colorful in photos.

The next day had been calm, hardly any water moving at all, and no others ventured out to the too-calm area but them. It hadn't even seemed like ocean water, more like pond water; the only difference was it was blue. Suddenly, there was a huge amount of colorful mahi-mahis swimming in the clear blue water. He and his friend had fished until they had all they were allowed. It had been an unusual day and boy, had he and his buddy Rick had a blast.

Still, his life was here, not off in the deep sea but here on the pretty lands of Texas, with a combination of rolling hills and flatlands because they were situated on the outskirts of hill country and flatlands. It was a great place and all their water spots had fish. It filled his time with fun.

He pushed open the door and grinned when Lumas, who sat behind the tall counter, looked up and grinned widely at him. Lumas was not a real heavyset man but he was a big man. He was around six feet or so tall, broad-shouldered, and probably wore a size eleven in boots. And they were buddies despite the fact of Lumas was old enough to be his grandpa their thought processes worked the same: they loved to fish.

"Hey there. I had to help, you know, get all you storekeepers up and going so you can welcome all your customers to town and give them a happy day tomorrow. I guess some of them will be here for the whole weekend if they're spending the night somewhere."

"Yep, it's always fun. And you're right, your new sister-in-law…no, let's see. Cousin-in-law. Is that what we should call her since her new husband is your cousin, not your brother?"

Ace laughed. "You're thinking the same thing I was thinking today. It's more like me and my cousins are brothers, so she feels more like my sister-in-law. But I bet you're right, she's my cousin-in-law. I guess we'll go with that."

"Sounds good." Lumas lifted his hand and a lure dangled from it. "I thought this would get you in here.

This here is an—"

"Old Bomer Speed Shad lure." The lure was old, probably made in the 1940s, and a great one. "I had a newer one than this but sold it." He grinned. "I'm glad to have this one."

"I thought you'd like it. And it's a little more expensive than your favorite Heddon Lucky 13 lure."

He hitched a brow. "Well, you know I love that one, and it's hard to beat."

"I know. I like my Heddon Lucky too, so you can just hang this on your cabin wall that has all those ancient lures dangling on it."

He laughed. "You know they're there. My walls have boards with rustic wood frames and when one gets full, I add another one. Yeah, I hang them all on those boards to look at but I always fish with them first. I'll study them some nights and then pull one down and head out the next day to fish with it. When I'm through, I hang it back up for decoration. So, how much is this one? I know it's not one of the cheaper ones." He and his brother had been overly blessed with a lot of oil on the ranch and cows. He was proud of the cattle and horses because they raised them. The oil—well, they just had it pumped and sold. The reality was they didn't have to have the ranch cattle, but they did because that's the way they liked it. He lived a rather simple life despite all the money in his heritage, and when he wanted a lure, he splurged. And he wanted to fish with this lure tomorrow morning.

He also knew that Lumas wouldn't cheat him and that when he said a number, and he did, Ace knew it was a fair price for the ancient, antique lure that grinned up at him as he held it in his hand and stared at the shiny, dark-gray spine, the pale-gray body, and the red eyes and lips of the lure with the hooks dangling from its tail and chin.

"I like it. It's going fishing with me in the morning."

"You know I give you first choice of all of these because I know you really do appreciate them and you use them like they were meant to be, then put them up for display. You don't just hang them up and pretend they didn't ever really do a job."

"I know. That kinda gets me, too, when people buy

antique things and just set them up to look at. These lures were created for use and brought smiles to people's faces when they helped them catch what they were fishing for. I want to feel that."

Lumas nodded. "Yep, we are alike in that. But I have to tell you that I haven't fished with this one. I don't always use them before I sell them to somebody, as you well know, so you're getting first dibs. Anyway, I had other things on my mind this week. With the dance coming along and well," he grinned, "my granddaughter is coming to town, and I had to get ready."

"You have a granddaughter?" He figured it was the one in the photo. By the look on Lumas's face, this was an unusual thing—someone coming to town to see him.

Lumas took a deep breath and patted his fingers on the counter. "Yeah, I have a granddaughter. She just turned twenty-six, same as you. And we've never been around each other since she was a little girl. Her daddy, my son, coped with the loss of his mother differently than I did…and we had a fight a long time ago." He sighed. "He hasn't had anything to do with me since then. But while I could, I sure enjoyed Kelsy when she was little—it's not like I'm going to be telling anyone else this. But you and I are friends, despite the large age difference between us, and I wanted you to come by for this today because I need to talk to you."

"I'm glad you did. What can I do?"

"I don't really have anyone but her. I stopped trying to call my son after a while. We just don't see eye to eye, so I finally took his hint and left. I've sent gifts to her on her birthdays and Christmas, but I don't know if her dad gave them to her or if I'm ever mentioned to her anymore. Well, the fact that she's actually coming here makes me think he did tell her something…or maybe she remembers something because she was about eight in the picture I keep on my desk, and that was the last time I saw her. I always hoped she would remember me and one day I'd see her again. I've just prayed all these years that the good Lord would keep her safe around all those bulls her daddy rode and now raises."

"And He must have answered your prayers."

"When she called me out of the blue, she told me she was coming and would like to stay awhile if I would let her. She told me she'd quit her job and was looking to try life in a small town. That's what she told me. She didn't go into detail about what led her to want to do that. But she and her parents lived most of her life on the outskirts of Dallas…you know, on the land, but next door to the city. A little different than out here in the good ole boonies."

Ace smirked. "Oh yeah, I know. I prefer the boonies anytime." He hated the city.

"Me too." Lumas laughed. "Anyway, she said she quit her job and is arriving tomorrow, if that was okay with me. I said yes, of course. I even told her she could have any room she wanted, I was going to be so happy to see her." His blue-gray eyes grew brighter than Ace had ever seen them. "And then I told her she could work here since it was going to be hers one day. That if something had happened to me, she was going to inherit this and some other things. And she seemed kind of startled. I mean, would you be startled if your grandma and granddad left you something? A little or a lot, grandparents and parents have things they want to share if they can. Of course, love is the most important thing…and that's what I'm ready to do again. I've always loved that sweet girl."

Wow…he could tell this was really a strong emotion-filled conversation for Lumas, who wasn't the strongest talker in all the world. Ace understood now that some deep hurt ran inside Lumas, and that was one thing Ace understood. The two of them had more in common than he'd ever thought. They had pain in their lives and they used fishing to ease it up.

"I'm really sorry about what happened with you and your son, but I'm here for whatever you need me for. I'll help out any way you need me. I'll tell her what a great man you are, and you don't even have to give me a good deal on a lure." He grinned and Lumas did too. "You are—you know you are. Me and you might not be the same age but we think a lot alike."

"She's going to get here about mid-day, so I'm not coming in to open the store. The party is tomorrow night, and I already told her we were having a big dance in town and if she's wanting to live here in this little town, it'll be a good time to see that it's not a boring place, that we do have things to do. I also told her it'll be a good time for me to introduce her to all my friends.

She sounded excited about the prospect, and that made me happy. I really do think she wants to live in a small town. I don't know what happened but I'll find out. All I know is that tomorrow my life is about to change." He grinned and his eyes sparkled. "I get to spend time with my granddaughter." His voice had grown wobbly—the strong, big man got tears in his eyes.

Ace swallowed hard. "Well, I can't tell you how excited I am for you." And he was, but he still wasn't sure what he was supposed to do. "So, ah…you just want me to be nice to your granddaughter? Is that what you want?"

"I don't have to ask you to be nice to her—you already are nice to everyone. But I was just wanting you to know so when you see me walking up with a young woman tomorrow night, you'll know who it is. And maybe you can, you know, come up and talk to her. Maybe ask her to dance. Just help make her feel welcome here. Maybe take her fishing sometime—I don't even know if she likes fishing, but she's a cowgirl maybe. My son was a bull rider, a rodeo guy. Yeah, he rodeoed. That's one thing I never talk about, but me and

Millie have a little bit in common where that comes into play. But not exactly the same. Well, okay, a little along the same lines."

Ace's mind whirled. *So Lumas had a son who'd been a rodeo guy.* And obviously Lumas didn't like that. Millie, who was an amazing rodeo gal, had married a bronc rider and had been happily married. He remembered the day he was helping Dustin build the goat pens at the B&B, she was helping plant flowers and how nice the woman was but she'd also been single for a long time. Her bull-riding husband had died and she'd walked away. Hid out there on her place, then came to town, opened up her resale antique store. And though she still wore one of her many shiny award-winning buckles, her boots, jeans, and Western shirts, as far as it was known, she'd never ridden a horse after leaving the rodeo circuit upon the death of her husband. Nor dated anyone—despite the fact that older men in town watched her and probably wanted to date her. But no one had tried. She was clearly not open to it.

Suddenly, it slammed into Ace. "Your wife, who passed away before you moved here, you never talk about her. I'm guessing she was a rodeo competitor? Did she ride? Did she get killed in a rodeo?" Why that had suddenly jumped into his mind was because Lumas had said he and Millie had something in common; had they both lost the loves of their lives to the rodeo?

Lumas took a deep breath. "Yeah, she did. And I wasn't there to try to save her. It was a crazy weird thing. She was killed by a raging bull and she wasn't even a rider. My son was a rider but wouldn't quit even though one had killed his mom. Bulls were and are his life—he raises them. Rough bulls. And that's what I just couldn't take." He sighed heavily as he looked away.

Then he picked up again, "He was furious at me because I kept asking him to stop doing what he loved. I'd lost his mother to a bull, and he was the one doing the really dangerous event—I knew I could lose him. But he told me if I couldn't deal with it to walk away. And so, I did. We happened to be in Marathon, in the Florida Keys fishing—because he enjoyed fishing too. And you saw that picture of me and Kelsy on that pier, the one in my office, that was our last picture together because me and my son, Olsen, had our argument right after that. I got in my rental car, drove to the airport, and flew away. And I actually haven't seen him since.

"How do you tell someone you're sorry about what they do and when you think about it, your heart hurts? It's terrible. I loved my wife, and I knew when I married her what she did. But, when rodeo killed her, I couldn't handle it anymore. She was in an area where she should have been safe, picking up her hat that had fallen off in an empty area, so she jumped inside to grab her hat. In the next instant, a bull blasted into the pen and took her out. It happened quickly, rough and brutal. So, I guess I just couldn't understand why my son, who knew that bulls were the cause of his mother's death, kept riding them and raising them. Still kept putting his life on the line just simply by putting his boot legs on the bull's back and settling in for the ride."

Ace was stunned by the story and could understand Lumas's worries. And the son's determination to hold on to what he loved, despite losing his mother. "I'm so sorry for what you've gone through."

"I'm sorry for what you've gone through too. But now you know the story that no one in town knows. I hope you don't go spreading it. I trust you, but I thought since I'm asking you to help watch out for Kelsy and befriend her that you needed to know what was between us in our family. And I felt like since you lost your mom and dad that maybe you'd understand and be there if she needs anything."

Ace was struck by the whole telling of the story. Before he could stop himself, he reached out and placed his palm over Lumas's clasped hands resting on the desk. He squeezed. "I'm here however you need me. You weren't here when I lost my parents but soon after I lost them, and I had no idea you'd been through a similar trauma. I don't know if I've ever told you but your shop, fishing and finding lures here, enabling me to get out there in the quiet, helped me. Still does. Not going in to detail, but fishing is a soothing way to get your emotions in order. Or to be distracted." He pulled his hand away and stuck them in his jeans pocket.

"I thought that might be the case. Now you know why I understand because this is where I disappeared, too. Fishing, doing the thing that I love. Fishing and looking for old fishing lures to sell. To share with people. Yeah, standing on the shore of a fast-moving river or a calm lake or creek bed—it's all wonderful. To me, even a raging river is peaceful because your thoughts get lost in the water when it goes rushing by."

"Yeah, you and me—it's almost like we're the same person in so many ways. So I'm buying this lure and in the morning, I'm going to test it out. Then, tomorrow night, when I get to that dance and see you, I'm going to tell you and your granddaughter how it worked. And then, if she seems like she's having a good time and needs someone to dance with, I'll ask her. And you know I don't ask a lot of women to dance."

Lumas chuckled. "I've noticed that. It makes me know you won't take advantage of my granddaughter. I didn't think you'd do that anyway."

He pulled his wallet out. "I wouldn't, but I'll be there if she needs something. If she needs to talk, I'll be there because I understand. And I kind of like the idea of helping if I can. And who knows…maybe there is nothing about why she's coming here that's sad. She might be thrilled and happy to come here and live with you. Sounds like she loved hearing about the dance." He laid the money on the counter.

Lumas took the money and tapped the keys on the ancient cash register. When the drawer opened, he counted out the change and handed it to Ace and smiled. "Thank you. Okay, now, you take that lure and you catch us a bass. Hopefully a big bass."

# CHAPTER TWO

Kelsy Camry tapped her fingers on the table in the bakery where her best friend worked. Her best friend who got no credit even though she worked her rear end off, making sure the bakery had great food and service. She was up early at four in the morning and inside the bakery, making sure all the morning delights were ready for the six a.m. customers. Her boss was an overpowering, arrogant fella who took credit for everything, saying he'd taught her and her dad everything they knew. But Kelsy knew if Violet wasn't here doing most of the baking and making sure it was done right, this place would not make it—unless he hired someone new to take her place. He never came to work these days, and Violet worked really bad hours. So, Kelsy figured if she wasn't here, Mr. Smartypants would be in a bind, and she personally wished her friend would put him right where he belonged.

He mistreated her friend so badly, but there was Violet, always trying to do her best, knowing that one day she would have her own bakery and would leave the dude behind. But Kelsy knew that wouldn't be for a while. Violet felt like she owed the man for what he'd done to help her father—his celebrated baker—after he'd been hit by a car and now was limited to a wheelchair. She had stayed to take her father's place and was very grateful to Mr. S for letting her fill in, considering he couldn't work there anymore. As madding as the man was, making Violet work such long hours, she felt she owed him for helping her and her dad stay afloat when he was in rehab and in their time of need.

Kelsy's story wasn't quite so tough. She'd always wondered what had happened to her grandfather. And then, one day, she'd been looking for something in the attic, and she accidentally knocked a box off a shelf and it hit the floor. The top flew off and a mass of colored envelopes landed around her feet.

She knelt and, to her astonishment, they were birthday and Christmas cards from her grandfather. She realized that her sweet granddad, who she had so loved and enjoyed fishing with, had been sending her these, even though her parents hadn't given them to her. He'd been sending them every year as usual. Before she was eight and he'd left their last fishing trip, she'd seen him on all the special occasions. But then, after he left, she hadn't seen him since. But he'd been sending her gifts.

Her parents had just hidden the fact from her.

Her dad had told her, when she asked all those years ago, that they wouldn't be seeing him anymore. And that had basically been the end of talk about her grandfather. She'd lost her grandmother and her grandpa within a few months, and in the short time she'd had her grandpa after her grandmother's death, he'd not been the same happy man he'd been before. That had been apparent even to her at the young age she'd been.

But she'd asked her dad again and angrily he'd told her he was gone and she'd never see him again. And she hadn't but then she found the cards. And her anger went to her dad rather than her granddad.

Five weeks ago, she'd found those cards, cards where he wished her a happy birthday and Christmas and wrote things like he hoped she enjoyed the gifts…what gifts? She found no gifts in the attic but he'd obviously sent them. He'd sent her birthday cards and gifts, Christmas cards and gifts, and she'd seen none of it.

Not any of it.

After getting hold of herself in the attic, she found her parents and had a little discussion—a confrontation.

And she'd decided it was time to make choices of her own, and that meant she was headed to the little town of Lone Star, Texas, that Granddad had told her about in his later cards. She'd have wanted to see him even if he lived in the middle of a city.

Violet came and sat at the table. There was no one in the bakery right now because it was after the morning rush. Her delicious muffins, kolaches, breakfast pastries, Danishes, and homemade biscuits filled with eggs, bacon, or sausage…her delicious list went on and on, and were so wanted and craved by everyone that the place was really busy. Busier than it had ever been before Violet took over the baking.

"So you're really packed up and leaving in the morning?" she asked, her beautiful face drawn with concern.

"Yes, I am. You know I haven't been happy ever since I got that business degree that I'll probably never use. Then I found those cards I told you about from my grandfather. I loved that man so much. My goodness, I've missed him. And then to find out that my dad kept so much from me on why he disappeared… I really don't know what happened, but I cannot go on and not find out. The man who I felt loved me so much ran off and left me and then, well, I just haven't found my place, haven't been happy. Then I talked to Granddad on the phone, and he sounded so much like I remembered and he was so thrilled to hear from me. and that I was coming to visit." A tear slipped from the corner of her eye, and she swiped it away.

Violet reached out and placed her hand on her arm.

"He even told me that the fish store he owns will be

mine, as well as everything else he owns. The man hasn't seen me in all these years, and yet I'm inheriting everything. It just doesn't make sense. He's been building a fish business in that little town. He says it's a lot of antique and old fishing tools and lures, but also new too. I remember how much he liked to buy old lures and fish with them. So it makes perfect sense that he went into the business. He loves lures. It fits. And I was only eight, but I remember all of that. I'm trying to comprehend everything that's happened, that's gone on that I know about and don't know about. So…yeah, I'm going. And I'm really looking forward to it. And I'm going to a town outdoor party tomorrow night. They've started having them for all the storekeepers' customers and anyone who wants to come. He's excited because he can introduce me to everyone, and he says I'll love it. Or he hopes I will."

"It sounds wonderful. What about a job?"

She smiled. "He brought that up and said I had one at his place, but if I didn't like it, there were other places I could work at. I'm looking forward to this and maybe after I get out there you'll come visit me."

"Maybe."

"I looked up this lady who he told me opened an online store and it was a huge success, so she came there and made it her home and opened a real store in town and it's helped the town so much. But, he said maybe that we need an online fishing store. Anyway, it all sounds great. She's the one who got the dances started, and all the cowboys in town are enjoying the chance to get to meet people and dance a little. It just all sounds fun, and inviting. Me and Granddad have to talk but he sounds wonderful, and I'm going. So I'm here to give you a hug and to tell you goodbye. I'll be calling when I get there. If you have any problems, call me. He said the house has plenty of room, so if you wanted to come visit, there's room…"

"I'll try to figure out how to take off and do that. But are you staying?"

"I know I'm doing something different. If it doesn't work out there, then I'm finding somewhere to start over. Somewhere that puts a little distance between me and Dad, because I know he's not going to like it when I tell him where I'm going."

"You haven't told him or your mom?"

She shook her head. She'd been hesitant and decided, at her age, she could make decisions on where to go that had nothing to do with her dad. It sounded awful but needed. So needed. "I'm in disagreement with them, but I'm sure I'll come home for a visit at some point. It's not like I'm ending my relationship or my love for them. It's just time for me to step out. Maybe I can somehow reunite my parents and granddad. This is a new episode opening up in my life, and I want it to be a good episode. So I'm going into it with a positive attitude."

Violet grinned at her. "You're going to do amazing. Okay, I know you've got things to do, and I have to get back there and bake some cakes. But I'll be missing you and looking forward to your phone call. Keep me posted. I'm interested in that dance you're going to tomorrow night. I'm still in awe about the woman who started the dance."

"Me too. Her parents traveled all over the world and took her along, and she was tired of it. Her mom had gone to Lone Star when she was a kid on vacation with her mom, and so she went to see it and fell in love with the town. And then a man." She grinned. "And she opened a physical store and invited her online customers to come to the real store. If they come, she takes her picture with them and posts it on her website. It's interesting how she drew customers like that.

"And then the dances started, inviting the town's customers and that's where I'm going to be tomorrow night. Oh, and I actually bought a dress from her online. Not that I have any place to wear it, but I couldn't help myself. At home, I wear boots, jeans, and a tank top to work. Maybe I'll wear it to the dance tomorrow night. Anyway, as you see, I'm excited." She hugged her friend. Oh, how she loved her friend and hated leaving her, but everyone had to deal with their own lives. And though Kelsy believed it was time for Violet to open her own store, that wasn't her decision. They both had to find and make their own way in life, and Kelsy was ready.

And so looking forward to it. She hoped—no, she wasn't going to hope—she was going to be determined to make things work out. And if they didn't, it wouldn't be because she hadn't given it her all.

~*~

Ace had had a great morning fishing on the river with his new/old lure. It had worked awesome and might not make it onto his lure display anytime soon. He had a bucket full of fish that he'd clean when he got home; he'd put them in his ice chest to keep them good until that time. And thank goodness for the ice because, as he pulled off the dirt road from the river and onto the paved country road that ran a long distance along the ranch frontage, he spotted a cow and her baby in the middle of the road.

He pulled onto the grass, put the truck in park, then hopped from the truck to the grass. His fishing gear was still on; his coverup and wet boots that had kept him dry when he'd chosen to walk out into the water now didn't quite fit the job. But he had his cowboy hat on, and he pushed it back from his forehead a bit as he looked at the mother and calf. The calf that was drinking from its mom right now, smack in the middle of the road.

He looked around and saw a red truck in the distance, giving him a few minutes to scan the fence line. He spotted where the barbed wire was down, in a spot on the schedule to replace. That was going to have to be fixed today. Thankfully there were no other cattle in sight, because mother cows didn't always stick tight with the herd when they had a newborn. The baby had probably been slower getting used to the terrain and they'd lingered back, or one of them had found the opening and the other had followed.

He looked up the road. The truck was getting closer, and he knew whoever it was had plenty of time to spot him. He was fifty feet from the mom and calf, being cautious because he didn't want the baby to run. The mom was used to them working around them but the new calf would be different, and he didn't want them to get run over. He turned toward the coming truck and waved his arms. He had automatically put his flashers on since they commonly had cattle finding their way out onto the massive roads winding about their large acreage.

Thankfully, the red truck slowed down. As it eased his way, he realized it was a woman driving. A young woman. As she got closer, he saw she was a pretty woman. The song "Pretty Woman" started playing in his head. His mom had been a huge fan of Roy Orbison, and he and his brother had heard many of the singer's songs. He smiled, thinking of his pretty mom and now, looking at this younger woman. Everyone knew that old song; he listened to country music but still had a love for Orbison's music because it made him smile, just like it had made his mom smile. And he still remembered watching his mom and dad dance together to some of his tapes…his mind instantly went to how, back then, he'd wished he could one day find what his parents had. He'd been ten when they died and been thinking things like that. Things he no longer let himself think about.

The lady pulled to a halt. She wasn't dark-headed like Julia Roberts, who played in the movie *Pretty Woman* with that music setting the scene. No, this woman was blonde. She let her window down, and he mentally slapped himself on the cheek as he strode to the window as she stuck her beautiful head out and smiled. *Holy smokin' tortillas, the woman was pretty.* Her blonde hair was long and slid over the window's edge to swing free as she leaned out. It had a hint of cinnamon mixed with honey to it and glistened in the sunlight.

"I see you have a mama and a baby feeding in the middle of the road."

Her smile tickled through him like feathers—he wasn't sure whether it was butterfly wings or bird feathers or chicken feathers; it was just feathers floating all around him.

"Yeah, I just pulled out from the dirt road you passed back there, and I found them. This is our family's ranch property on both sides of this area, so she's ours. There is a messed-up fence down there where they got out. We'll be getting that fixed quickly. But sorry, we have to wait just a minute—I hate to interrupt the feeding. Hopefully when the baby stops its feeding, I'll just walk over and herd them back through the fence and you can move on."

She was staring at him now. Her eyes were beautiful, the color of fresh spring grass with an edge of gold to them, bringing out the soft freckles that ran across her tanned cheeks. She was awesome, and he was at a loss for any other way to describe her.

"I hope I'm not making you late for something."

She propped her elbow on the door and her cheek on her knuckle. "No, not really. I'm driving through here, looking for my granddad's place. I'm coming for a visit. May even move here."

He froze. "Are you Kelsy Camry?"

She straightened up. "Yes, I am. How did you know?"

"Well, as you can tell by my outfit, yes, I'm a cattleman but also a fisherman. I just got through catching a bunch of fish with an old but new to me lure that I bought from my very good friend, your grandfather, yesterday. When I was in there buying it, he told me you were coming. This is the strangest thing, that we meet like this."

*What in the heck was he saying?* He was acting as

if he were in one of them romance movies his mom had loved. She might have walked out for a minute and left the TV on, and he'd get stuck in the middle and would finish watching it with her when she returned to find him there. That was then, but even now when he sat and scrolled through the channels, he would pause to watch one and remember the good times.

"Well, that's wonderful. I'm so glad you know my granddad, and I'm so excited to get to finally see him again. I drove down another road and then came to this one and honestly, I'm lost. Does he live somewhere near here?"

*Man, she had sparkly eyes. And a great smile and energy too.* And no doubt about it; she was excited to see Lumas.

"He lives down here. You just have to go past the cows, after I move them, keep going a few more miles, and on the right side of the road, you'll see an iron fence entrance and a mailbox. His mailbox is a large bass fish. So when you see the bass fish mailbox, the bass with a big mouth, you just turn in and drive down the lane. He has a few acres, and you can see his house up on a small hill. Your granddad is excited that you are coming to visit him. And I also need to tell you that he is a great person. I am very glad to call him my buddy even though, as you can tell, there is a few years' difference in our age. I'm crazy about Lumas. He can find me the best fishing lures, like the one I bought yesterday morning. He saves them for me if he thinks I'll like them."

Her smile opened wide. "I guess we have that in common because I love to fish, too, and I got that love from Granddad. I can see how you and him are great—well, I don't mean to say something when we just met, but that was the first thing I thought when I saw you wearing your cowboy hat and your fishing outfit."

He laughed. "Yeah, I look like I'm a hard-riding cowboy, don't I?"

"Yes, or a fisherman. Anyway, I'm going to go find my granddad. I told him I'd be there—well, I guess I better wait till you get your cows fed and moved. Looks like the baby has stopped milking."

"Yep. Give me a minute and I'll herd them to the opening, so as soon as they are off the road, move on by slowly and then head to Lumas's place. I know he is excited and waiting to see you. And I hear that y'all are coming to the town dance tonight. He'd asked me if I'd come meet you, so he'll be surprised that I already have."

"I'm glad to have met you first. And I'm so glad to hear that he's doing good. It's been a long time since I saw him, and I was kind of worried—anyway, a long story but thanks. Because I have a feeling that if you like him, then he's still a great guy."

# CHAPTER THREE

Kelsy watched the amazingly good-looking cowboy in his fishing outfit topped off with that straw cowboy hat as he moved toward the mama and baby. He spread his arms wide, and they tromped in the direction he wanted them to go. The man wasn't crazy; he didn't have to wave his arms. It looked as though he might be talking to them as they trotted away. He waved his fingers every once in a while when they'd look over their shoulders at him, but then they'd keep on moving down the slope to the ditch, and then up and right through the opening in the fence he herded them toward. A couple of times, he'd stepped to one side, keeping them going straight and not detouring. He definitely knew what he was doing. She watched the cows go through the fence and then realized as he turned and waved at her that she had not pressed the gas pedal and had not moved forward like he'd told her she could do.

Knocking her head mentally against her steering wheel, she gave him a real wave and moved forward. Unable to stop herself, she looked into her rearview mirror and saw that he had moved through the fence opening too. She assumed he'd move them deeper into the pasture so he wouldn't have to worry about them coming back out before he could get the fence fixed.

*She was going to see that fella tonight.*

As much as she was startled and surprised, she was looking forward to it—not that she'd come here to have a romance. This was about her and her granddad at first. But there was no denying that if that fella asked her to dance, she was going to.

Moments later, she saw he had been right. There was the good-sized bass mailbox, with its tail curved up and its large mouth ready to be opened when her granddad opened the lid for his mail. It just made her smile seeing it. She turned down the drive. It was a red dirt road that led toward a mid-sized wooden home with a wide front porch, oak trees, and his old truck parked in the carport. Like fishing, he also liked old trucks. This one had a curved cab, a short bed, and was the color of an orange sunset. Her smile widened. She noticed that behind the house was a small pond and she wondered whether he fished there or went other places. She figured that, like the gorgeous fisherman-cowboy, there were probably lots of places out here where he could fish.

She couldn't stop thinking about the fella and wanted to know his name and before she really thought about it, she knew she was wearing that pretty dress she'd bought online from the owner who had the store in town. The woman who was helping the town get customers to come to town to have a good time shopping and a great dance.

As she pulled to a stop in the small circle drive, her granddad stepped out onto the porch. He grinned huge and strode from the porch toward her. He wore his jeans and a T-shirt that had a bass on the front; her heart thundered and a grin blasted across her face. *Granddad.*

Unable to stop herself, she was out of her truck in an instant and hurrying toward her grinning granddad.

He threw his arms open wide and embraced her the moment they reached each other. Standing there on the stone pathway, she burrowed herself into the arms and chest of the man she always remembered being so strong and welcoming. The man she'd thought she'd lost, and now here they were together again.

"I missed you," he said against her hair.

She sent a prayer up that this was not a dream and that nothing would come between them. "Oh how I've missed you." She looked up into his glistening eyes.

"I'm so sorry things worked out the way they did and I haven't been in your life."

She tightened her hug, then stepped back. "I'm not sure what all went on between you and Dad, but hopefully it's not something that will affect us. And to be honest, right now I don't even want to talk about it. I'm just happy that you are doing well and are obviously happy. On the way out here, I was looking for your home, and I came down the long road and I met a fella. He was standing on the road, guarding a momma cow and her baby that was feeding. He stopped me and said y'all are friends. He had on fishing clothes and a cowboy hat."

He grinned widely. "You met Ace, my buddy. There's a big age difference but that kid—man, I really like him and I'm glad y'all met. I had approached him yesterday to help out tonight visiting with you so you wouldn't feel left out or anything. And he'd promised he'd come say hi to you and maybe dance with you if you needed a partner."

*Ace*. She grinned. "I hope you aren't trying to fix me up."

"Oh no, no. That's not what I'm trying to do. I just didn't want you to come here, not knowing anyone, and so I asked the fella who I like a lot and is about your age to help me out. I figured that he could at least come talk to you."

She didn't tell him that she'd been teasing. No, she wasn't expecting him to fix her up after they hadn't seen each other all these years. But why had she said that? She wasn't sure. "So where do we start with this new getting to know each other? There is a lot to talk about and we will, but I want to see your house now. I love it out here. I really do."

~*~

"Millie, you sure do look good this evening. You ready to have this party?" Josie Jane Willis asked. She was the owner of Josie Jane's Wash and Repeat store, and she was excited about the town dance they'd been getting ready for all afternoon.

Her tall buddy, Millie, loved the dances they'd started having, too. She'd gotten more involved in the dances than she'd ever been about anything since leaving the rodeo behind after the death of her bull-riding husband. She was about fifteen years younger than Josie Jane, and Josie couldn't help but have her brain stuck on hoping the right man came along and drew Millie out of the hole she'd dug herself into after losing her first husband.

Now she stood behind the dessert and drink stations, like train track stopping gates, while she watched everyone else have a good time. Maybe one day she'd come out from behind that table, and Josie Jane wanted to be around when it happened.

"I didn't do anything different. I got on a pair of

dark jeans and one of my champion barrel racing belt buckles and my red checkered Western shirt." She grinned. "And of course, my boots. I love some bright boots. So what's wrong with all of that?"

"They're great." Josie Jane grinned. It was true; Millie always wore fairly the same thing: jeans, Western shirts, champion belt buckles, and boots. And today that was the changer. She had on a cool pair of white boots, with flowers on them—Texas bluebonnets and the Indian paintbrush the main flowers. The boots were colorful and looked good on her long legs with her jeans tucked into them. She was in her early fifties and she was just a great, beautiful, strong woman who Josie thought hadn't had the happiness of a long, wonderful marriage like she had known, or their good friend Ruby, who still had the life and love of Red. She and Ruby both had had Millie on their minds.

She'd helped them get the area for the dance ready, and Josie Jane had seen a lot of the older and not-so-old fellas watching the lady. They'd also tried to offer her help, but Millie thought she could do everything on her own, and she pretty much could. But as far as Josie saw it, she'd be doing herself a favor to accept the offered help from the men who were looking for an opening with her.

However, maybe this endeavor to get these dances going to draw attention to their town would also draw attention to her sweet friend, the rodeo-award-winning gal who'd married a bull rider and lost him too soon. She'd quit her rodeoing and come home, and as far as any of them knew, she'd never rodeoed again.

She'd been a big help getting the town ready for these dances, and the other day she'd gone out to help newlywed Sydney Buckley plant flowers at her big house, the new B&B in town. Josie Jane and Ruby had gone out to look at it yesterday, and it looked wonderful.

"Well, I hope the dance goes great like the previous ones have been," Millie said.

"It sure is, and it's wonderful to see all these people so excited to come to our little town."

"I know. And I heard from Beatrice Ratcliff that she was in Arabella's bakery this morning, and Lumas Camry came in and picked up an assortment of Danish and cookies because his granddaughter was coming to town and going to stay for a while, and maybe even stay. He's bringing her to the dance tonight."

"Really? You know, that man doesn't talk much. Our stores are fairly close to each other since mine looks across the street and down the road that his sits on. With the way the incoming road makes a T right there, everything that goes on at his place is in my view—if I'm looking in that direction. Anyway, he comes to his store and stays there. He doesn't hardly come out unless he comes to one of our town meetings."

Josie Jane studied her friend. "Yeah, I noticed that, but my shop isn't as close to his as yours is, and you do have a good view down that road. So you watch what he's doing a lot?" This was very interesting. One thing was sure: Millie was a tall woman, and Lumas was taller than her…they'd make a good set. *Why had she never seen that before?* Because neither of them appeared to be interested in finding romance—she better think about this before she made a huge mistake.

# CHAPTER FOUR

ce arrived at the dance early. He didn't normally arrive at the dances early but today he did. He walked over to the dessert table and drink table where Millie Watts and Josie Jane Willis stood, and Ruby Mulberry just walked up before him.

Millie grinned at him; he liked this lady. Josie Jane watched him with interest, as did Ruby. All three of the ladies were nice and working hard to get people to come visit Lone Star.

"Hi, ladies," he said. "How's it going?"

"It's going fine," Millie said. "We're looking forward to having a great dance tonight and plenty of folks out there dancing. Are you going to dance?"

Josie Jane spoke before he could. "I heard the rumor that Lumas has a granddaughter in town and that she's going to be here tonight. Maybe you need to ask her to dance. You know, make sure she gets to dance with someone."

He crossed his arms and laughed. "Goodness, ladies, I think I might do that. But, see, Lumas already asked me to ask her to dance. He wants to make sure that Kelsy doesn't feel left out or anything."

"Kelsy," Josie Jane said with a little drawl and a smile. "So you already know her name—"

"I know her name because Lumas told me she was coming yesterday when I went by and bought a new lure. He's excited. He hasn't seen her in years. Did y'all know that?"

"No, actually," Millie said. "He's been here all these years but he's a quiet person and doesn't say much. I'm sure in his shop it's different but, around town, not so much. He just has his shop and works there. I've seen him go to the diner sometimes, but usually he heads straight home. I assume he fishes most of the time when he leaves work."

Ace studied the tall, pretty lady, his curiosity suddenly up because she knew so much about his buddy

Lumas. His single buddy who had been single ever since he'd moved here. Ever since he'd lost his wife. He'd never seemed to take notice of anything other than fishing, his shop, and lately the dances and gatherings they were having. So the fact that she noticed so much about Lumas had Ace's interest up.

"So, okay…yes, I had noticed that, and he's going to be here tonight. It would be really good if all of you ladies go over and make his granddaughter feel welcome. He loves her very much but he hasn't seen her in a very long time. I'm asking y'all to do this because I know y'all are all very caring ladies and you'll naturally make Kelsy feel at home. Actually, I happened to have met her earlier today when I was leaving my fishing hole. You know I fish every time I get the chance, just like Lumas, and that's why we're buddies. I had a cow and baby out in the middle of the road that I was about to usher off the road and back through the gap in the fence. The baby was nursing, and I was waiting for them to get finished when Kelsy drove up. She was nice, and I told her where her granddad's place was, and for her to look for his big ole bass mailbox with his mouth ready to open up and eat the mail." He laughed and so did Millie and the other ladies.

"That is one special mailbox," Ruby said.

"I've always thought it was funny how that bass looks like it's ready to chomp down on all of his mail."

Josie Jane grinned broadly. "I have a feeling that once you told her about the bass, she didn't miss it because it's really easy to see."

"Yes, ma'am, and I'm pretty sure she found it and will be here tonight. So are y'all going to do that for me?" He focused on Millie, wanting her more than anything to go over there and start talking to Kelsy and Lumas. His brain was working like fire, thinking about what a match those two might make.

"You can relax because, yes, we'll make sure to get right over there," Josie Jane said.

The woman loved the idea of matchmaking, and he figured her mind was working and once she and Ruby got their eyes on Kelsy, they would instantly be wondering who they could match her up with. It suddenly hit him in the face that most likely it would be him. He was already the one set up to ask her to dance but he couldn't worry about that right now. He had no plans to ever marry, they didn't know that but it was the truth. His past hurt too much to even think about that. But he could be nice and help that beautiful, really beautiful, woman out. Actually, he was looking forward to dancing with Kelsy.

She'd be his one dance of the night…it hit him suddenly that maybe if he got the chance tonight, he'd dance with Kelsy twice. But he doubted that would happen because once all the other cowboys spotted her, she'd have fellas piled up, aiming to ask her to dance. So, he might get to dance with her once if he made sure to be the first to ask, because he knew she was going to get asked a lot. When those soft green eyes of hers slammed into a fella and with those golden freckles on her pretty cheeks, topped off with a smile—those guys were going to line up like she was the queen of the rodeo, and the one who danced the best would win her— not that he was saying that was how it would go, but that would be how they'd be thinking and want in on the competition. He'd never been involved in that but he'd watched the fellas drill in on certain ladies before, and it seemed like a competition. Tonight, thankfully, Lumas had already lined him up and he'd get the first dance, if he asked her before anyone else. He wasn't going to worry about everything else. He was just going to be there if she needed anything and to help watch out for her, just like Lumas had asked him to be.

He planned to greet them the moment they showed up. He could use the excuse of telling Lumas about the great success the lure he'd sold him had been. It was still in his fishing box and not going on the wall any time soon. For him to take that out of his fishing box and hang it on the wall, Lumas was going to have to find him one better. But, then again, that lure was what Lumas used to get him into his shop so he could talk to Ace about his granddaughter. So that lure was worth more to him than what he paid for it. It was a lure that was helping him to do something to help his friend. To help Lumas achieve something he really wanted, and that made Ace smile.

"You sure are smiling." Millie grinned back, hitchin' an eyebrow at him.

"Yeah, I was just thinking about the fishin' lure

Lumas sold me yesterday. Y'all know how I love to fish and he gives me the first opportunity on lures he thinks I'll be interested in, and I can say I went to the river this morning before I met Kelsy on the road. Anyway, I had a bucketload of fish I caught when I met Kelsy this morning. It is amazing. It was a good day all around, so I'm going to let y'all have a good time while I walk around and say hello to a few others."

With that, he turned and walked away—trying not to run. Something on the face of those ladies as he was talking told him that their minds were clicking, and clicking fast. But he couldn't worry about that.

This was for Lumas, and he always did what he told someone he'd do.

~*~


Kelsy loved her granddad's home. It was nothing fancy; it was just him. It was neat and had large furniture, because he was a large man. It had been put together in a "live in me" kind of way: Leather couches that looked years old and well broken in. There were a lot of fish on the wall that he'd caught and had mounted. And then there were several fishing tournament trophies because he'd once been big in that community. Her heart had seized up tight when she started seeing her pictures…so many pictures of her sitting all around the house.

All the rooms had pictures of her. The table with a lamp on it at the edge of the living room. And the counter in the kitchen had several—some of her, some of her and him, and there was even a picture of her, her mom and dad, and him. This told her that whatever had happened that caused them not to see him after all these years, he still kept a picture of his son close. Right there in the kitchen where he'd see it every morning and any time he was there. And this gave her hope.

He had been so happy to see her. They'd talked about all they were going to do and the party tonight, where he could introduce her to all his friends. And then, after they'd visited for a while—never talking about what had driven him away or her coming there— they'd talked about their time together before it had all split up. It brought back such wonderful, sweet memories…oh, how she'd missed this man. Finally, she'd told him she'd go get dressed and asked him what kind of clothes did women wear.

He'd smiled. "Well, you just wear whatever you want to. The women come from all over. We have our town ladies; some of them are dressed up and some aren't. One of the ladies, she used to be a rodeo champion and she dresses…well, she wears boots. You never know what her Western boots are going to look like. They're usually fancy. She was a national champion in barrel racing, making it to the NFR, and she wears jeans tucked into her boots and a pretty Western shirt tucked in, showing off one of her many award buckles. Then there is Ruby. She and her husband run the diner. And Ruby wears things that she tells everyone she bought at the new store in town, Genna's Classy-Sassy Boutique."

He chuckled. "What a name. And I know this only because Ruby talked about her clothes at one of our town meetings. She's a…what they call a full-figured woman, and she looks good in what she buys from that store. You might want to go try the store out—though you'll look pretty in anything you put on, but Ruby is colorful and not Western like Millie.

"So, there is going to be all types of clothes there. Everyone isn't a cowboy or cowgirl. I'm certainly not. They're all people from every walk of life who enjoy coming to our small town and shopping for the day, looking for things from the past and now having a dance with good music, refreshments, and maybe meeting a new friend. But a lot of them come for Genna Barry—now Buckley's—store. That store is online and no telling how many dollars' worth of clothes she sells online. It's a humongous worldwide business, and she chose our little town to settle in and call home. She's wonderful and immediately fell in love with West Buckley and all of his goats. I'm going to have to take you out there one day. They have some really cute goats. Have you heard about them?"

She grinned, charmed by what he said and his enthusiasm. He loved his town. "Yes, I have. I read her articles and I actually have a dress that I ordered from her online store that I was thinking about wearing tonight. Do you think it's all right to wear a dress?"

"Honey, I think you wearing a dress would be a

great big hit. Not that I'm telling you to start dating the cowboys, but I can tell you that our little town has a herd of great young men. And they love to dance. In particular, I already asked Ace to ask you to dance. I just wanted to make sure you didn't feel left out—not that I didn't think you weren't going to get asked. Now that you've met him, you can dance with him, then probably have a line waiting to dance with you. But if you don't want to dance, you just tell Ace, and he'll make sure he and I take up your time. That will give you a nice way to not have to do what you might not want to do. It's all up to you. I can already tell you that all the ladies in town are going to come like a herd over to meet you."

Her heart thundered. The want to giggle a bit—and she wasn't a giggler—but her granddad was looking out for her in a wide open way and it touched her deeply. She was no longer a little four-year-old, a five-year-old, six-, seven- or an eight-year-old or a newborn he'd held when she was first born. All the memories she had from the age of four and up were great; he'd always looked out for her. And he was doing it now. And it felt wonderful.

"Okay, then I'm going to wear the dress because I ordered it but have never worn it. Because, well, you know I grew up on a bull ranch, cleaned stalls, and well, just didn't have a place to go and wear a dress. So tonight I'm going to wear the dress I ordered and love. And, by the way, I love the way my room looks. It's such a beautiful room. It reminds me of Grandma. She loved teal and the minute I walked in, I chose it because of the teal-tone bedspread and the inviting fluffy pillows. I know that's not you, so you must have had her on your mind when you decorated it."

He nodded, taking a big breath. "Yep, she loved that color and so did I. It matched her eyes and, well, I told you that you could have any room in this house but in my heart of hearts, I felt like that was the one you'd choose. It has a great view of the lake and a nice bathroom and all the flowered rugs. And your pictures, too. I need to tell you that I don't hide your pictures in bedrooms—I put them out here for anyone who comes over to see when I have visitors. But the truth is I don't have them much. I work at the store and then I go fishing, so there isn't much time left to invite people over. Very few have ever been in my house, so the pictures are for me and I've enjoyed all of it. Anyway, I put pictures in that room of you and me and us and Grandma. I just wanted you to see what I think about when I look around my house. And a…"

His words stumbled, and Kelsy's heart clenched tight because she knew he was fighting off emotion.

Her great, big, wonderful granddad was fighting back tears. It dug so deep, so very deep that she wanted to cry too. But she didn't want to press things on her first day.

"Thank you. I love it. You did great. I know Grandma hasn't been with you for a long time, but she would love this house. Truly. All right, I'm going to get dressed, and we can head to town. I'm eager to meet your friends more than I'm interested in dancing."

He grinned again. "Well, believe me, they're going to come up to meet you. You know, I've never been a big dancer…danced a few times with your grandma. The beauty could dance. And she and your daddy danced, and I know at a tiny young age, she taught you, so don't not dance because of me. Personally, I'd enjoy seeing you out there dancing and having a good time. At least take a dance with Ace. Okay, he's a great guy and I can tell you that he's not going to put any kind of pressure on you.

"That boy doesn't date. He and his brother live here in town with his cousins and uncle and aunt because they lost their mom and dad. Not long before we lost your grandmother. He's never told me this but the boy fishes, he never dates and at a dance I've never seen him dance more than twice. And in all the years I've known him, as far as I can tell, I've never seen him dance with anyone more than once. So if you get that dance out of him, he's doing it for me. And maybe for you, since you're beautiful and he's already met you. But if you wangle a second dance out of him, I'm just letting you know what a triumph that is. I often worry about my good friend. I want him to move forward but I have a feeling he has no plans to ever marry."

Her grandfather's words about Ace struck her hard. *Why did Ace have no intentions of marrying?* She felt for him, having lost his mom and his dad at an early age. She was thankful that, yes, she'd lost her granddad—a huge lump filled her aching throat—but they were reuniting now and just knowing that Ace wouldn't get to do that here on earth made her even more grateful for this chance to start a life with her granddad back in it.

~*~

It hadn't taken long for people to start showing up. Everyone enjoyed the gatherings and dance. He was talking to his friend Chet, when he saw Chet's gaze shift and his expression looked a bit startled; then a smile curved his lips as he looked past Ace's shoulder. Ace turned, pretty much knowing what he was going to see before he saw her.

And when he saw her, he froze. She had on a pretty dress, the beautiful green-toned color of her eyes…his heart did a rampant slam against his ribs and his pulse went rabid. Her gleaming hair hung over her shoulders, the soft tone of blonde blending beautifully with the soft flowing dress that the gentle breeze ruffled about her knees. And his gaze locked on her pretty legs and the flat pair of sandals she wore, showing off pale pearl toenails—

*What was he doing!* He yanked his gaze back up to her face. And fought hard to get his brain off how stunning she was.

No, she wasn't what some would say was the most beautiful woman in the world, but she was to him…he slapped his head on the inside. *Get it straight, Ace.*

Then, as he stood there, watching her walking with her granddad, he excused himself from Chet and forced his feet to walk before everyone in the world bombarded them. And he met them as they made it to the edge of the gathering.

Lumas grinned at him, and so did she. They looked similar, in very different ways: he was a large built man and she was a small woman, but when they smiled, it came out that they were definitely kin.

He grinned too. "Hey, y'all made it. I'm glad y'all did and well, I—you told your granddad we met, right?" He was stumbling all over his words. Something was wrong with him.

"Yes, I did," she said, a chuckle in her words. "It's good to see you *again.*"

"I thank you for helping her find my house," Lumas said. "She liked my big bass out there on the road, and she and I are going to go fishing. She's a good fisherman, in case you want to know that."

Ace saw encouragement in his friend's eyes. "Well, you know I like to go fishing, but I'm not going to barge into y'alls first fishing trip in a very long time. I saw that picture of you two in your office. Y'all go and have fun. And go anywhere on the ranch you want to, as usual."

Kelsy laughed too. "Y'all think alike."

"Yep, this dude is my buddy." Lumas grinned. "I sold him a new—well, an old but new to him lure yesterday. How did it work?"

"It was awesome. And you know I have a lot of them displayed on my walls, but it's not going up. It's still in my tackle box. I caught a ton of bass today. And if it works that well all the time, it may never make it to my wall display. So you keep me in mind on lures similar to that one."

Kelsy looked from him to Lumas. "What kind of lure was it?"

"Old Bomer Speed Shad," he said, seeing she was

still a fisherman…woman. He grinned and she did too.

"Oh my, Granddad has one. I remember it after all these years. I can't wait to see yours."

"So that's how you knew how good it was. Well, thanks for saving it for me. And you can go fishing with me anytime if you love it that much, to remember a lure after this many years." They stared at each other; his interest spiked as her pretty gaze merged with his.

"You're welcome," Lumas said, his voice penetrating Ace's tangled-up thinking. "Okay, so I know you already said no, but how about you go fishing with us tomorrow?"

He swept his gaze from Kelsy's. "Tomorrow is Sunday, and I'll be going to church, then I'll be feeding the cattle assigned to me. Then, well, you know me…if there's time before sunset, I'm going. But you two need to enjoy your first trip out alone."

"It's up to you, Granddad, but if you'd like to go to church first, I'd love to go too. But for tomorrow, I'm good with whatever you want to do."

# CHAPTER FIVE

He watched as the ladies he'd asked to welcome Kelsy to town came toward them. They were moving fast and zeroed in on Kelsy. There was a small group of them. Josie Jane Willis led the way and Ruby Mulberry walked beside her, as did the very tiny Arabella Samuels, who owned the bakery. And behind them, Millie Watts. They were all grinning.

But with curiosity, he kept his eyes on Millie. He saw the tall, pretty lady's gaze go from focusing on Kelsy's face before looking up at Lumas—tall, broad-shouldered Lumas. She'd lost her husband years ago and though the men in town were interested, she wasn't. But now, he saw her gaze linger on Lumas. He was thankfully standing in a position where he could shift his gaze from one to the other, and sure enough, he saw

Lumas's gaze meet hers, linger, then shift away to the other ladies. *Was he interested?*

He looked back at the lanky woman who might be in her fifties; the beautiful lady had spunky red hair that waved softly around her face and just below her ears. He smiled, remembering how his new sister, no cousin-in-law Sydney had said she'd talked with her at West and Genna's wedding and she'd helped her move forward with the love she'd felt for both her deceased husband and Dustin. For that, he would always hold Millie in his heart, because whatever she'd said about love and loss had helped his cousin find love and be the man that Sydney and little Hazel needed.

*What did she need?*

There were plenty of women who were stunning all their lives, but the way he looked at it, it wasn't their build or their face or their shape that made their beauty—it was the warmth and caring in their eyes, and their smile that came from their lips. His gaze shifted to Kelsy. *She was all of that. Again, what was he thinking?*

Thank goodness he didn't have to speak because Josie Jane came up with a huge grin. She was short and tiny, as was Arabella. Ruby was more full-figured but not much taller, and then there was long, tall Millie. They made a great group with their welcoming smiles. They had it all. He grinned.

"Darlin', we are so happy to hear that you've come to visit your wonderful granddad," Josie Jane exclaimed as she came to a halt and the others did too. "He is an amazing man, though not the most outgoing fella. We love him anyway. We're thrilled that you're going to be visiting him for a while—or maybe forever. Anyway, I'm Josie Jane, and I own that store over there. If you need anything or you like to look at things that are old, fixed up, made shiny and new, come by for a visit. Or if you're not into that, this is my friend Ruby. She and her husband Red own Mulberry Diner—which is their last name and their place is the mulberry-toned store right over there. Wonderful food, just wonderful."

Ruby grinned but didn't have time to say anything as Josie Jane kept on talking. "Or, if you're in for wonderful treats, homemade cinnamon rolls, pies, cakes—all delicious—you can go into this sweet little gal, Arabella's, pastry shop. It's right down there on the corner, where the road into town meets a T. And then across the street, at the end of the T with a straight shot from her front window, down that street is this wonderful towering Millie Watts's store. It's similar to mine but we're good friends who root each other on. And she has a great view of your granddad's place on that side street."

This had been a whirlwind of introductions and like him, Kelsy smiled as her gaze went from each woman that Josie Jane's palm hand fluttered to as she introduced the ladies.

"It's so nice to meet all of you. I'm really thrilled to be here seeing my granddad after several years of not seeing him. I can already tell you that I'm so impressed with this town, the countryside and"—her gaze met Ace's, and a shot of lava flowed through him—"I met Ace right when I got to town and couldn't find Granddad's place. He happened to be watching over a mama cow and her baby who were taking up the road as she fed her baby. He gave me directions, and I really appreciated it. And to find out that they are fishing buddies was a neat surprise. And now I get to meet all of you and so far, so good. I'm excited about being here."

"Well, we are excited you're here," Ruby said, that well-known welcoming smile wide. "You come on over to the restaurant, and we'll all meet and have a good time welcoming you here. I'll buy you some lunch. And just so you know, there are a lot of ladies around your age here. We'll make sure you get to meet them tonight. Ace's cousins-in-law, Genna and Sydney, and the wonderful new hire at Genna's place, Jasmine. And Jace Calhoun from Calhoun's Feed and Seed—his wife Lila, who is also Josie Jane's granddaughter, is a wonderful young lady too."

"Yes, there are a lot of people for you to meet, and those are some really great gals around your age. While you're getting settled, come on over to my place, and I'll show you around and also buy you lunch." Josie Jane hitched a brow at her friend Ruby. "She's not the only one who can do that, you know."

Kelsy chuckled, seeing the teasing between the two friends.

Ace was enjoying this, and he could tell that Lumas

was too.

"I can't really compete with those two because they are very fun to be around, but if you want a good pastry or a piece of pie, like coconut or lemon, you just drop by my place and I'll fix you up. My treat," Arabella added.

"And I can vouch for all three of these ladies…" Millie interjected, "and the two wonderful places to buy treats. I like both places to eat at, so take turns and enjoy. In between all your eating, my place is in between the diner and the pastry shop. If you want to come in to visit." Her gaze went to Lumas. "Your granddad is a quiet person, but I'm sure that he is thrilled to have you here."

"Yes, I am," Lumas agreed. "I've been hoping for this day for a very long time. Thank y'all for welcoming her. As you can tell, she's a wonderful young woman and welcomed at the house for as long as she chooses to be here. So you ladies just keep it going. Make her feel welcome and help me out here."

Lumas's words had all the ladies grinning.

Millie's eyes twinkled as she said, "Well, in that

case, Kelsy might just get bombarded by all of us welcoming her here. But, we also don't want to run you off by being too friendly."

Kelsy laughed. "Y'all aren't going to make me feel too welcomed. I'm loving this. I just was ready to get off my dad's bull-raising property and explore the area where my granddad had chosen to settle. Now I'm really looking forward to visiting all of your shops and also to go fishing with my granddad."

Her gaze flickered to Ace.

"I might even get to go fishing with her," he blurted before he could halt the words. All eyes turned to him, and he was suddenly speechless.

"That'd be a great idea," Josie Jane cooed. "You are in love with fishing, just like her granddad. Do you like to fish?" she asked as her gaze settled on Kelsy.

And so did his.

"Yes, ma'am, I do. My granddad taught me well, up until I was eight. I fished with him every chance I got. And even after all these years, I'd sneak off to a creek down on our land and though the fishing wasn't great, I still enjoyed it. I'm so looking forward to getting back to fishing with him. And he says that Ace is one of the best."

"I wouldn't be taking that to heart," Ace said, fighting off his words coming out as a stumbling jumble.

"Are you saying what Granddad said isn't true?"

Everyone was watching them. He really couldn't help his next words. "Well now, your granddad is probably the smartest man I know. He knows his fish and his lures, and that little one I bought yesterday was awesome. It thrilled me and made my day. When I go fishing with you, I'll bring it along to see what you think."

She hitched a brow. "Sounds like a good plan. And we can have a challenge on who can use that lure and catch the most fish that day."

They stared at each other, and Lumas cleared his throat. "If you two are going to do that, then Kelsy, I guess I'm going to have to pass you mine that matches his and then y'all each have one and can fish at the same time and not have to pass his from hand to hand."

Kelsy's smile widened. "Then the challenge is on.

We'll keep all you sweet ladies in on how it goes."

Ace wasn't sure whether she realized what she'd just done, but he knew. He didn't even have to let his gaze flicker around to the ladies because he didn't want them thinking he was worried or anything. But it wasn't the fishing challenge he was worried about; it was what was going on in all their brains in that moment.

Music started in the background; the song was one he loved and was now up and going. Before he could stop himself, he did what he had been asked to do. "Kelsy, would you like to dance?"

# CHAPTER SIX

A tingle rolled through Kelsy as her teasing of Ace suddenly felt more like flirting than teasing. And it was undeniable that all the ladies had taken notice. The music of Brad Paisley surrounded them, and Ace looked a little like he was startled by what had just happened. But she shook off the worry. The awareness that they were now being speculated about couldn't be helped.

She took a breath and then almost instantly nodded. "Thank you. I think I'll dance with you since that was yours and Granddad's plan all along."

"Now, honey, that wasn't my plan for you to dance if you didn't want to. But I thought Ace asking you might help you if you were wanting to dance. I can see it's going to be a fun night, and that's what I wanted you to have. I have a feeling from the looks I've been seeing that you might get asked to dance a lot. So don't you worry about me. I'm going to visit with my buddies and get me some dessert. Now, you come find me when you want to." He gave Ace a look that tickled her. "But I'll be watching. I know Ace will be, too, so go on and have a good time."

She almost laughed, even though she should have been a little shaken up by all these people thinking they were fixing her up. Well, they weren't; they just didn't realize it. She wasn't here to be fixed up. Not for a while, anyway.

She slipped her hand into Ace's that he'd held out to her. She made sure that there was no show of emotion on her face, nothing to say she felt a hot tingle shoot through her as their hands touched and her heart raced. She kept her face clear, despite the fact that the sparks were still shooting through her from touching him. No, she was just going for a friendly dance with a guy, a man who had vowed to her grandfather to take her out. To introduce her to everyone and to help her have a good time. And that was it.

As Brad sang his hit, the great upbeat song, "Long Sermon," which she loved, she walked beside him to the area where the couples were now moving along to the upbeat song. At the edge of the dancers, instead of turning to her, he kept going, leading her through the dancing couples. It was clear to her that several cowboys were also interested in a dance with her, as her granddad had suggested. Before they'd gotten among the crowd, several had popped their hat from their head and nodded at her; others had tapped the edge of their hat brim and smiled. Now among the couples, she stopped looking at anyone and focused on the tan hat that sat on Ace's head and the sandy-brown hair curling at his nape.

She tried not to think about the way her fingers felt in his or the way those heated fingers itched to toy with those slight curls in front of her. No, she was determined that tonight was going to be a fun night. She was going to make it be that way. She would dance every dance she had the opportunity to join in on. That way, all those darling ladies—and anyone else who might be thinking that she had come to town and they were going to match her—well, they would have no idea by the time this night was over who she might be interested in. Yep, that was her plan.

They reached a spot among the other dancers, and Ace turned toward her. The song was about a fella wishing the sermon would end so he and his girl could go out and enjoy the day on a boat. And she realized—as he lifted their already clasped hands almost shoulder height, their elbows touching; then he slipped his free arm around her waist—that she was ready to get into the rhythm of the song with this good-looking cowboy/fisherman and dance. She made a mental note to try not to listen to the fun, smile-inspiring words Brad was churning out.

She noticed Ace made certain there was distance between them. He was being a very good gentleman. Either that, or he also knew they were being watched very closely. Then again, she was thankful he'd led them into the middle of the crowd so that anyone watching them would have to watch really close to see them talking, much less think something was going on between them.

She pushed those thoughts from her mind and smiled at him. "I like this song. And you are a good dancer," she said as they slid smoothly into step with the others moving to the music. Thankfully, this was not a slow two-step or she might have been in trouble.

"Thank you. I enjoy dancing and this happens to be a favorite. As you know, I love being out on the water. And like he's singing, tomorrow after church sometime, that's where I'll be, and you and Lumas will be too."

She smiled, unable to help it. How perfect this song was for him and boy, she hadn't been kidding—he moved as if they were on ice as he led them around the floor in complete rhythm with the song. "That's the plan."

He met her gaze. "I have to say, you dance good yourself. I don't really dance that much but I enjoy coming and watching everyone have a good time. Everyone invites their customers, and the crowd keeps growing. Before this, we just had community dances, and I'd come to them to stand around and visit with everyone. I normally dance maybe once, or sometimes twice. I'm not always known to get out on the dance floor. And why I'm saying that, I have no idea," he said, his brows dipping beneath his hat brim.

That was interesting. This amazingly good-looking cowboy with the incredibly good attitude didn't dance that much…that meant to her that he might not date that much, just like Granddad had told her. If that was true, she wondered why. "You're a kind of a stick-to-yourself kind of guy?"

Their gazes met. *Goodness, he had great sky-blue eyes, with a hint of aqua around the edges. High cheekbones. His hair…not too dark, with a little curl around the edges— What was she thinking?*

"Right, so, don't take that personal. I mean, your granddad asked me, and I do dance some—"

"Very well, I might add."

He smiled. "Thank you. I had a good teacher. My mom. She loved to dance, and she always danced with me and my twin. I'll have to introduce you to my brother Hunter and all my herd of cousins who we live with." He paused. "Well, my mom and dad died in a car crash when we were ten, and we moved over to live with our uncle and aunt. But my mom was a lover of dancing, and some of my best memories were of her teaching me to dance. I loved it, too, and even that young, I'd burn up a town dance floor with her smiling down at me."

He smiled, and she could see the sadness there despite the humor and love of his words. It touched her deeply.

"So, now, even though I don't dance a lot, I do get out here some."

Her mind reeled. He'd lost his parents, both of them, so early. Again, she'd thought she'd lost her granddad and then been given the gift of him being alive. "I'm so sorry for your loss. I hate that for you." She smiled tenderly. "But I can tell you that your mom would be proud of you. I don't know that I've ever danced with such an easy flow as this, and it comes from the way you lead." And she was not lying. They were moving around the dance floor as if they were on ice.

As she said those words, his hand that was loosely on her back spread out, and she wasn't even sure he realized that he'd pulled her a little bit closer. Instead of being nervous about it, happiness flowed through her.

"Thank you. But I have to tell you that you dance

well too. That may be why we're dancing this smoothly together—because, yeah, I noticed it as well."

Her heart warmed. *Goodness, this guy…what was it about him?* "Well, I'll just say that, um, I enjoy the dancing, and I am glad that you volunteered for this duty."

He paused their steps momentarily. "I don't exactly consider it a duty." His smile widened. "I'm having a good time, and I can tell you from the looks on all the cowboys' faces as I brought you out to the dance floor that they're all hoping to get a dance with you too."

"Well, I'll just be open and tell you that I'm not here looking for romance, at least not right now. I'm here looking to revive my relationship with my granddad, whom I haven't seen in years. So, I'm probably going to dance a lot tonight and hope that makes it clear to everybody."

His smile widened. "Then we're on the same page. Because as much as I'm enjoying getting to dance with you and getting to know you, I'm not looking for anything. I don't know if your granddad told you anything more about me, or even if he notices it, but I'm not planning on ever getting married. So I'm not the one to ever be romancing anyone. I'm just out here dancing with you and having a good time. I'm glad to meet you, and rooting for you and Lumas to have a great bond. Oh, and yeah, I'm looking forward to our fishing challenge." He grinned.

The man had a way with words. He'd told her bluntly, clearly, what his plans in life were. He didn't even ask her whether she was interested in having a romance and falling in love; he just made clear where he stood and that he was here just to dance with her because he'd promised his buddy, her granddad. So they were definitely on the same page, and it was a good place to start. They could be friends and they could fish together. And then walk away.

~*~

"Hey, little cousin," Caleb said as he walked up onto the sidewalk.

Ace looked at his older cousin. He was next to the oldest of his cousins, with Ryder being a year older than him. But of all his cousins, Caleb was the most muscular built. Unlike him with his thinner build and leaner muscles, Caleb's shoulders were broad and his biceps bulged at all times. But the cowboy's favorite thing to do growing up had been to wrestle cattle and still, when they were herding or someone needed help with a cow, he was the first one in the ring and could grab the horns and have the animal flipped over and on its back in seconds. And he thought it was fun—and fun was one thing Caleb was always up for.

As Ace looked into his flashing green eyes, he fought off a smile, just thinking about all the things Caleb had gotten into over the years. And looking at him now, Ace knew there was something on his mind.

"So you're not dancing right now…what's up?"

"Me not dancin'—well, I decided to take a break since *I've* been dancin' all night long. You, on the other hand, danced that first dance—yeah, I noticed. You and that pretty gal who I now know is Lumas's granddaughter…well, y'all looked like you were enjoying yourself more than I've ever seen you enjoy yourself. But you haven't gone in there and interrupted all that dancing she's done with practically every cowboy here tonight. I know, you never dance with any girl twice."

Ace didn't, hadn't, and never planned to do it. He wasn't doing anything that was going to get him hooked on someone. He wasn't taking that chance. And it wouldn't be fair either to dance with a gal again and again and maybe she started having a crush on him, and in her heart she was thinking him dancing with her meant there was a chance of them having a future together and that he might be her future husband. Nope, it wasn't him, and so he wasn't going to do that to anybody. Not that he was the best pick but there might be someone out there who thought he was likable and maybe want to marry him. So he wasn't risking that and he wasn't going to talk about it either.

He'd talked more about that to Kelsy during their dance than he'd ever talked to anyone about it. And he didn't know why he'd done that. But anyway, he'd made himself clear to her, and the minute their dance was over, she'd shown him that his choice hadn't meant anything to her by accepting the first offer to dance again as they were heading off the dance floor. And then she'd accepted the next dance with someone new, and then the next and then the next, and she was still out there dancing.

She was having a good time, and it was clear to everyone. That beauty had a smile and obviously loved the dance floor.

"Look at them over there." Caleb nodded toward the other side of the street, and Ace's gaze followed the direction of his nod. "Those three look happy, don't they?"

There was no not knowing who he was talking about, because there stood his cousin West with his arm draped around the shoulders of his wife, Genna. They were smiling as they stood beside Sydney, his cousin Dustin's new bride. They were all watching Dustin dancing with Hazel, his new bride's daughter. He loved them both very much and it was clear that they loved him too. That little girl could dance and they all knew now that she'd learned to dance with her dad and loved it and him. He'd passed away a couple of years before they moved here.

Ace's thoughts instantly flew to his mom and how he had danced with her from toddler age until he was ten and lost her. He realized Hazel had that special bond and could now enjoy it with Dustin. And he knew that Dustin cherished the child and was glad he could stand in for her daddy, and he treasured it.

Ace looked away, his throat clogging up. He'd lost his mom and dad way too early but he dealt with it. He threw his feelings into getting away and fishing. The peace of being out there alone, with nothing to worry about but watching the water and listening to the birds sing. The peace surrounded him as he stood on the banks with his lure and his pole. He'd loved running cattle and raising them like his dad had.

His thoughts again went to Kelsy and her reuniting with her granddad. He was so happy for them, and for Hazel out there dancing with his cousin. He sighed. He'd often thought how he never wanted to be like his parents—or Hazel's daddy—leaving loved ones behind. The emotion was overwhelming.

He knew his cousin hadn't just come up here for nothing. He knew he was watching him. And it helped him know that he was making the right decision for himself. He didn't ever want to leave someone behind and more than that, he didn't ever want to be left behind. So, he enjoyed his life alone.

He looked over at Caleb. "So why are you watching me like that?"

"We all know that you set yourself apart, and I can't say anything because I like to dance with everyone. But I'm not ready to settle down like those four over there. And that cute little girl would make anybody happy with those smiles. Matter of fact, she told me the other day that she was going to get me to dance with her but she's been having too good a time with her stepdaddy, so I haven't asked her. But I think I will pretty soon. It'll be neat to get to dance with my little niece. Anyway, for a little while out there, you looked different than you do when you normally dance with a gal."

He tried to not let that bug him. "Well, you know me and Lumas are good friends. We both love to fish, and he asked me to look out for his granddaughter. You know that not every fella she's dancing with out there is a good guy. You know most of them are but a couple aren't the best in the world. Yep, they live around here, and I can tell you he knows who they are, and so do we. So that's my job. He didn't actually point it out to me but as I've been standing here watching and I see the way they're watching her, I realized what he meant when he asked me to be around for her. So, that's my job and what I'm doing."

"Are you sure that's all you're doing?" Caleb studied him. "There's nothing wrong with you maybe wanting to go ask her to dance again. Lighten up, man. I know you and your mom used to love to dance, just like Hazel and her dad loved to dance. I remember. Y'all have that in common. Dustin knows it too. Why do you think he invited you to come over and help build that new goat fence? He knew that you and Hazel have that in common. Hunter has it, too, but he doesn't love to dance as much as you do. And yet he gets out there and still dances. I don't, and it makes me ache for you. You're a good, happy fella. You know your business. But anyway, I thought I needed to come say something to you.

"And I have to say, not to change the subject but to

ease it up so you don't think that's all I'm thinking about, these dances are working out great. You see all these ladies who are coming to the dance, and you see their fancy pants and dresses. I think they came from Genna's online store or they came here and bought them. But they look great. I even heard Josie Jane and Ruby talking, and that pretty dress Kelsy is wearing came from her online store."

"It's pretty." After he said it, he needed to fix it. "Genna has a way of making everybody look good. Look at Ruby—that woman looks gorgeous in that sparkly red blouse with those white pants that have that silky look to them. And look at her glittery sandals. So yeah, I'm enjoying watching everybody. The old, the middle-aged, and the young. These dances are awesome, but I'm still not joining in any more than I already do. But hey, thanks for your concern."

His cousin lifted his shoulder, his eyes sparkling. "I'm not going to push you. I just thought I'd give you a nudge. But anyway, I'm off to find me somebody else to dance with. And no, I'm not going to ask Kelsy to dance. I don't want to make you jealous like we did with

Jace and that pretty gal he married, when we all danced with her that night when she came back to town. And it kind of boosted him to take action. We're not going to do that to you, brother—yeah, I know you're my cousin but I love you like my brother, so I'm just wishing you'd…dance more." He hitched a brow and his gaze went back to Kelsy coming off the dance floor once again. He grinned. "Go guard her. Call it what you want, but you know you want to ask her to dance again."

And then he was gone, thank goodness, and Ace was left alone to watch Kelsy obviously tell one of the dudes he didn't like no; the man frowned then walked away, and she headed toward her granddad. He headed that way too. Needing to let Lumas know he'd been watching out for her like he'd been asked to do.

# CHAPTER SEVEN

Kelsy had danced the night away. She hadn't been exactly sure why she'd felt she had to do that but after her dance with Ace, she realized she was attracted to him—whether she wanted to be at the moment or not. Then finding out that he had no plans to ever fall in love—well, he'd made that statement and his words had stayed in her mind—*I'm not planning on ever getting married. So, I'm not the one to ever be romancing anyone. I'm just out here dancing with you and having a good time.*

He'd made it clear that what he was doing was for her granddad and had no intention of coming in between their friendship. She'd actually hoped that from all those cowboys who had asked her to dance that one of them would make her heart flutter and her pulse race like it had when Ace had taken her hand and sent a shot of heat flooding through her as he led her out onto the dance floor. Never had she experienced that sensation.

It wasn't just a physical, internal feeling of her arteries acting crazy or her pulse increasing…it had just been cool. Different. Unforgettable.

But she would forget it. Oh yes, she would. And she would just be friends with the amazingly good-looking cowboy. As she had come back to her granddad to let him know that she was danced out, he had laughed.

"Well, sugar, me and my friend here, Bo Calhoun, who owns the feed store and loves to fish, we enjoyed watching you out there having a good time."

*Oh goodness.* "Nice to meet you, Mr. Calhoun."

The man, about her granddad's age, smiled. "Call me Bo. And yep, we enjoyed watching you. It's great to see all our grandkids enjoying themselves."

"Yes, it is," Granddad added. "I had a feeling you weren't going to have a problem getting a dancing mate so, as usual, that cowboy coming our way gave you his one dance, and y'all looked like y'all had a good time on that single dance."

"That fella and his one dance, maybe two dances, and never with the same gal," Bo added.

She turned and saw Ace coming their way. Once again that little sizzle went through her nerves as she watched him approach, tipping his hat to people as he passed them and said something to him. But it was obvious he was coming their way.

"Yes, we had a nice dance. Y'all have a wonderful friend and like both of you, fishing is his thing."

Both men grinned.

"It's been nice of him, helping me get used to things tonight."

"He's a great fella, that one," Bo said. "I'm going to go find my grandson and his fairly new bride and maybe get me a dance." He tipped the bill of his cap and then headed off.

He seem very nice but she was glad that it was just her and her granddad who would be chatting with the approaching cowboy. "So everyone knows about his single dancing."

"Yep. Everyone paying attention sees it. Like Bo said, one, maybe two dances but never with the same lady twice. So, honey, that might have been the last time you dance with that cowboy. Ace is a man with his own mindset."

She hitched a brow. "And I think y'all do well together."

Ace came to a halt in front of them. He smiled an easy smile, nothing flirtatious, nothing suggesting that he was attracted to her, just an easy smile at her granddad and then her. She tried to make sure there was no attraction shining in her eyes as she looked back at him. She had control over her life, and it was going to stay that way.

"I tell you, you took me out there and you danced with me, and then, boy, the night went by fast. I've never danced so much in my entire life."

He grinned, his lips widening a bit. "I knew that was going to happen, and I hope you had a good night. A good dancing night."

"I did. And Granddad seemed to have a good night, talking with all his buddies."

"Yep, enjoyed visiting with everyone," Granddad agreed. "So, Ace, how about you? Did you have a good night tonight? You stood over in the shadows over there most of the time but for you that's not abnormal. You usually stand to the side and watch everyone else have a good time."

He shrugged. "I mostly come to watch and talk. Y'all know that. And I talked with my cousins Dustin and West and their wives before I went across the street and took up my spot. Caleb came up, and we watched them having a good time. That little Hazel loves to dance."

"I noticed that," Kelsy said. "I passed by them several times when I was dancing and that little gal loves to dance."

"Yeah, she lost her dad a few years ago. They moved here not too long ago and, well, Sydney and Dustin fell in love, and sweet little Hazel targeted him as her new dance partner—that's what she and her dad loved to do. So Dustin loves it and it's cool when you see them out there having a great time. You know her dad is smiling from heaven, seeing the lights shine in her dancing, her smiles, and her eyes."

*Goodness, he had a way with words.* "I have a

feeling your dad and your mom probably smile, watching you stand over to the side like you do. They're probably wondering why you're not out there more than you are. But I bet it makes them smile anyway." He held her gaze and she wondered if maybe she'd hit on something.

Her granddad shifted from one foot to the other. "Maybe you should try dancing one last dance with Kelsy before we head home. That'd be two in a row and unusual."

Ace's gaze darkened a bit. "No, sir. I'm heading home. I just came to tell y'all goodnight and make sure Kelsy had a good time. And if y'all come to church, I'll be there, unless we have an emergency with a cow or a horse. I already had to fix that spot on that old area of fence down from your place." He'd gone straight back out there and repaired the fence after putting the cow and calf back in. It hadn't taken him but a few minutes to repair it before getting dressed and coming to the dance. "If I don't see y'all in the morning, I know you'll have a great day tomorrow and catch a lot of fish. Y'all haven't seen each other all these years, so your first time fishing together since that picture in your office…y'all will have a special time. It was nice meeting you, Kelsy. And I know for a fact you'll enjoy yourself. Your granddad is a great man and an amazing fisherman."

She leaned into Lumas's shoulder and slipped her arm around his waist as she hugged him. "I think so, and we're going to have a great time tomorrow. I'm looking forward to it. I have so many wonderful memories."

He smiled, but it seemed tight. "I'll see y'all in a few days then." He tipped his hat, took a step back, then headed away.

Kelsy watched Ace walk away. *Goodness gracious.* That guy was tall, lean, and muscled. But there was just something about him, something just floating around him that said *I'm the man.* "He's a little different, isn't he?"

Granddad slipped his arm around her waist. "Yes, he is. But he is a great guy."

She had a feeling he was. Everything about him said it was true. And everything else about him said *don't touch me.* She had a feeling that meant *don't touch my heart.*

And she would heed that.

~*~

Ace strode into the large barn where they had their morning gatherings before they took off and did their sometimes individual jobs on the ranch or like today a group job of herding a large herd of cattle from one area to the next. He was ready to get after it, needed something to keep his mind where it kept straying off to.

Yep, three days since he'd been into town, he'd been working and fishing alone and making sure he didn't have time to go to town to pick up supplies or happen to see Kelsy. He knew he would at some point; there was no way of not seeing her again sometime soon. But he just felt like he needed to avoid that right now.

West looked up at him when he walked into the barn. He stood over in the corner where the coffeepot sat on the wide bar area, the gathering place for years before work began each day. "I was in town yesterday and stopped at Bo's feed store, and Bo and Jace were talking with Lumas. And they were talking about his granddaughter. I saw you dancing with her—your one dance the other night. Anyway, he said they had a blast fishing but he also said he wanted to bring her out to see the goats at our place. He said his back's been hurting a bit by the afternoon, and he was going to ask you if you'd bring Kelsy out to our place while he gets on his heating pad in his recliner."

Ace's brain worked hard, trying to remember the last time his buddy's back had hurt him. "Sure. She can't drive out herself?"

"Nah. Needless to say, he said you'd offered to introduce her to everything—I guess he means introducing her to our goats, too. Anyway, when you get time, after we herd these cows, maybe tomorrow you can go into town and talk to Lumas and Kelsy and set it up. He said she was working in the store now. You know me, I'm not a big fisherman so I haven't been in there like you are every chance you get. But me and Genna are planning on cooking supper for y'all when you come out. So maybe tomorrow evening after Kelsy gets off work. Actually, since Genna won't be working Thursday that would be best. Kelsy can see our cute goats, and we'll all enjoy a great evening. Genna already knows her. Kelsy came into her shop to tell her how much she enjoyed the dress she'd gotten online. I think she bought a few other things. They hit it off. They are around the same age, same as Jasmine, who is really helping Genna have a little time off, which I'm grateful for. So can you take care of that?"

He tried not to look alarmed. He *had* promised Lumas to help out. "Sure. I'll go into town in the morning and get it figured out. Anyway, I've got to check on Lumas and his back. It's been a long time since he had trouble with that back of his."

"Yeah, it has, but he also said when they went fishing, two days in a row, they did some heavy hiking, getting to some good places on the ranch. He thinks that's probably what did it." He grinned. "He also said he wasn't complaining, that he wasn't going to complain at all because he had had the time of his life with Kelsy. I think it's cool that his granddaughter came and found him. Man, he just seems happier now than he's ever been."

"I agree with you. In all the time I've known him and been buddies with him something's been missing and now we know what it was. I'm really glad that she decided to come and see him." He couldn't say more, but he knew whatever it was, Kelsy had proved to him to be a person who liked to take control of things. Coming to see her granddad after all these years was part of that. He felt like it would all turn out good. At least her granddad was alive, and he was glad she'd found him before something happened and he was gone. Lumas was a healthy fella, a large guy, but he took care of himself. The man hiked along rivers, ponds, streams, and lakes a lot, so the fact that his back was bothering him still kind of felt fishy to Ace.

He hated that he was thinking that but he did think that…it didn't matter, though, because he'd promised to help out, and the one thing Ace didn't back off of was a promise.

# CHAPTER EIGHT

They got busy after his conversation with West. They loaded up the trucks and headed out. Caleb drove and he was in the front passenger seat; West was behind him and his brother Hunter sat in the back on the driver's side.

Caleb looked over at him as he drove over the dirt road, crossing the big ranch and pulling the trailer with the horses behind them. "You know, when I was over on the south side of the ranch day before yesterday where that big stream is you like to fish in so much, well, I noticed the water seemed down. I was fixing a fence and noticed it. You think they're drying up?"

"It's not that dry. You know me—I'm fishing a lot and none of the places I've been at lately seem to be getting lower. I'll head over there on my next fishing trip and check it out. Maybe I'll catch a bunch of big fish. That's a great fishing spot. But yeah, I'll check it out and see what's up."

He wasn't going to say it, but the last time he'd fished down there, he'd seen a couple of beavers and if his suspicion was right, he had a problem. Hopefully he could take care of it. He was going to go take a look.

They reached the area with the cattle before them and everyone loaded up. This was the cowboying part of his life that he loved. His mom liked to dance and be a cowboy's wife, and his dad liked to be a rancher and be a dancing woman's husband. Just thinking about it made him smile.

He looked at Hunter, his twin with a very strong resemblance but still they were able to be told apart. "Every time I get on a horse, I think of Dad."

Hunter grinned. "Every time *I* get on a horse, I think of Dad. Goodness, we weren't very old when he first sat us on top of a horse. Poor guy—most men have one kid to teach at a time, but he had two of us. And if he put me on first, it made you mad and if he put you on first, it made me mad."

They both laughed, because it was true.

Their cousins had all gathered around on their horses.

Like the others, Ryder had a big grin. "I remember one time—of course, you two are ten years younger than me—so I remember when your dad brought y'all over to surprise you with the little tiny Shetland ponies he'd gotten y'all. He'd decided that might make y'all little toots happy. What, you were about six maybe?"

They all laughed.

Ace remembered and knew what was about to be said.

Ryder continued, "You, Ace, decided to spur it with your tiny little spurs and it went into a kicking and bucking fit, as little as the thing was. I will never forget watching you ride that little pony across the pasture and not getting bucked off. And you, Hunter…" He laughed and everyone else did too. "You thought it was so funny that you busted out laughing so hard we thought you were going to make your pony run because you were laughing and shaking so hard. But yeah, it was a scene. Everybody but your dad was laughing at that. He was racing as fast as his boots would carry him across the pasture, trying to catch up to you."

Ace grinned, loving the memory. "Goodness, you're right. I think we were about six when that happened. By the time we came to live with y'all four years later after they died, we were ten. And y'all know we could ride the heck out of a horse."

Hunter met his grin with his. "Dad was good, and he made sure we could do what he loved."

"Yes, he did," Ace agreed.

Zack took them all in with a sweeping gaze. "On that, we can say our dads were alike. Those two men loved horses. Of course, our dad still loves horses but he loves Mom, too, and she likes to travel. Y'alls mom loved to dance so like your dad always danced with her, our dad leaves the ranch to us and travels with Mom and they have a great time. But you know the first place he goes when they come home for a visit is on a horse."

It was true. Ace's dad and his brother had been brought up on this ranch like him and his brother and cousins. And they all loved ranching, sitting on a horse and looking out across all that land they were blessed to own and knowing they could ride all day if they wanted to. It was a special life.

And then there was all that money that happened when that oil had been discovered on their land. They were so stinking wealthy at first but their granddaddy, smart man that he was, had started buying land and cattle. He hadn't used the money to run off and party or enjoy life in a different way. He'd used the money to expand and they had all learned from his example. They had money but did they live like wealthy millionaires—nope. They lived to ranch. The money was a big blessing that they'd been taught could be used to help others, and that's what they did. They had their charities they gave to and they watched for other times to contribute. He knew his dad would be happy they'd carried that on.

He smiled at everyone. "Well now that we got that great reminiscing out, let's go do what we love and live to do—herd them to the other pasture."

They all grinned and nudged their horses at the same time.

The whole wide line of them spread out and they

moved forward together toward the large herd of cattle ahead of them. Ace knew now they looked like a grown, strong string of cowboys but he knew long ago when they were little boys, his dad liked to always say they looked like the cast from that John Wayne movie, *The Cowboys*. A bunch of very young boys had been recruited for a dangerous cattle drive when John Wayne's character had needed help, and there were no adults around so he'd gotten that group of boys together and taught them everything his dad and uncle had taught all of them growing up. That's what this felt like. They'd grown up early on the back of a horse, helping their dads herd cattle. And one day his cousins and his brother would all have little kids of their own, and they'd be teaching them the same thing…but not him. He wouldn't let himself.

~*~

"Okay, Granddad, I had a talk with Genna yesterday at her store when I went in and did a little shopping." She grinned, having really enjoyed herself. She liked Genna and her helper, Jasmine. "We talked about online business and she's really good at it. Of course, we don't have pretty dresses, blouses or pants like she has, but we have what many men and women love and that is fishing equipment, old and new. You and I both know there are a lot of people who love this. I'm amazed looking at your record books and the numbers. Out here in this little town, you draw people here. Yes, there are many wonderful places to fish in this countryside but they obviously detour to shop in this store. Those fishermen come and fish all over the place, or they agree to come along with their wives so they can spend time in here with you. I see your numbers are biggest on the weekend—well, Friday and Saturday since you don't open on Sunday. And we were out playing on Monday because you said it was your slowest day. It's awesome what you've done with this place."

He grinned. "I kind of take it easy but I love it. They all come in and we talk, and they buy and then fish. Sometimes they call me and ask if I have certain things and if I do, I get their credit card number and their address and mail it to them. I'll write it down and send it in. But I think you're right—we could have a great online business. And one day when I'm long gone, you can run it all. Even from this little town, if you decide you want to make this your home. And I'm going to be honest…I hope you do."

She'd been thinking about it. She'd been here almost a week now. She had a lot on her mind. She loved her granddad and was so glad to be here. But it still bothered her about what was wrong between him and her dad. And then on top of that, Ace Buckley kept popping into her brain when she least expected it. What was it about that guy that he wouldn't let go of her brain and walk away?

And as she stood there thinking about him, the door to the store opened and in he walked. And, of course, whether she wanted it to or not, her heart flew up against her chest like it was a bowling ball that had been thrown by a world champion. She even leaned forward over the desk, it hit so hard. His eyes locked with hers—she blinked and looked over at her granddad. She was going to get control of this.

"Look who's here," she said to him.

Granddad looked from her to Ace, and he chuckled. "We figured you'd be by eventually. I got some new lures in and saved one for you, but I didn't call you because I knew you were busy. I talked to your brother the other day and he said y'all were fixin' to herd some cows."

"Yes, that's what we've been doing. And you know me—I like fishing and herding cows. It was fun. Supposed to be work, but we all enjoy it. So, anyway, West told me that I'm supposed to take this gal out to see his goats. And that he and Genna are cooking supper while we play with goats. He told me you didn't want to go because your back hurts. So what's up with that? I mean, I'm happy to do this." He paused and looked at her.

She almost laughed but held it in as he looked back at her granddad.

"But I'm also worried about your back. You haven't had problems with that in a long time."

"No, but me and this little gal kind of overdid it those two days. Well, I did; she's fine. I took her to some of my favorite places. I don't know if you made it to church Sunday, but we decided since it's been so long since we've seen each other to go on out and we went early. We enjoyed ourselves and did it again on Monday. I just left the Closed sign up like I sometimes do, and we went fishing at some more of my favorite places. We climbed down some ravines and climbed back up them, and you know that's not good on an old back."

She hated that his back was hurting. But as much as she didn't want to say it about this cowboy, who wanted nothing more than to be a friend of hers, she wanted him to take her out to his cousin's place to see a bunch of cute goats. Actually, she couldn't wait. "If you don't want to go, you don't have to take me. I can go see the goats myself. But I do want to see them. They sound so cute. Genna also talked about them to me. And little Hazel and her mom came in while Genna and I were eating, and that girl loves her goats. So yes, I'm eager to see them—not that I'm getting any goats out on your place, Granddad, but I do want to see them having fun. And I'm talking with Genna about how to get an online store going for Granddad."

There, she'd made her situation clear…this was all about goats and business. Not about him.

# CHAPTER NINE

"You are…?" Ace asked in a drawn-out question after hearing her words.

"Well, she does have a business degree, and I figure if anyone can open a business for me online, she can do it. Besides that, it's going to be hers. I'd give it to her right now and I'd have more time to fish. Me and Bo over at the feed store are in the same boat. His grandson has eased up his time, though. So maybe you can do that for me." He grinned at her and her eyes twinkled, making Ace's stomach churn.

"Don't you say you might be quitting. I haven't said one way or the other if I'm moving here or not. But I sure can look into getting it set up."

Ace watched with interest. They were getting along great and were a little bit alike. He liked that. He sure hoped…well, he hoped she stayed for Lumas. He watched her eyes sparkle. *Oh man, her eyes were so beautiful.* She looked at him, and he forced himself to speak with clarity. "So, you want to go see the goats?"

"I do."

"Okay, so if tonight is okay, Genna's been off, so she's going to cook. Y'all can visit about your business and play with the goats. Their place is covered with them, and they love taking care of them."

She chuckled. "About as much as my granddad loves his fishing and you love your fishing?"

"You got me there. I do love it that much. So, how much do you like fishing?"

"I love it."

"Maybe," Lumas blurted, "while I'm down with my back, you can take her fishing. Matter of fact, why don't you do that? I know you're going fishing Saturday, you have those new lures."

He stared at Lumas; the man gave him a hint of a grin to one side. "Sure, I'm going tomorrow to the place on the far side of the south end."

"Yep. Good fishing along that flowing stream."

"Well, it's having a problem. Caleb noticed it and said it was down. So I'm going to check it out. He's not much of a fisherman so he had just asked why it was looking low. He brought it to my attention because he knew if anybody would know if the water was different, it would be me. So I'm going there tomorrow to check on it."

"You're the one to know if the level of water is good, bad, or ugly, so you're the one to ask."

He grinned at his buddy's words. "I guess I do have a reputation."

"Yes, you do. It is a pretty area though."

"Yeah, very pretty."

"If you're going out after lunch, I'd love to go. Fridays, Granddad's business picks up with the weekenders, and he says they spend a lot of time talking. So I think I'd like to leave it to them and go see the countryside. And help if I can."

What could he say to that? "Sure. I'm taking my canoe to go downstream so I can see it up close and personal."

"That sounds even more interesting. I love

canoes—used to ride in Granddad's. So it's been a very long time since my last ride."

"And she'll remember how to ride in one."

"Okay, we have another plan. I'll pick you up this afternoon about five-thirty."

"Sounds good. I'll probably wear what I have on since I'm going to play with goats."

She chuckled, and he enjoyed seeing those sparkling eyes light up again.

"Well, you look nice right now—maybe too nice." She had on white jeans; he could see her crossed leg sticking out to the side of the register desk and her sandals had no strap around her ankle, just dainty slide-ons. Her blouse was a bright pink and a material that asked to be touched. She looked beautiful to him—just how he didn't need her to look.

~*~


"They are adorable," Kelsy said as she climbed out of Ace's truck the moment he'd put it in park at the old ranch.

Ace had picked her up like he'd said and driven her out to West and Genna's home. It was down a dirt road, had a Texas flag mailbox and a large red barn beside a beautiful old white ranch house that his granddad and grandmother built. He smiled over the truck after he'd also climbed out. She was excited and oh so beautiful.

"They're everywhere. And look, those three are standing on those two donkeys' backs."

Ace chuckled. As much as he had tried not to look forward to this moment, he had thought about it off and on all day. "The goats and those donkeys get along well. The donkeys don't mind being the main attraction for this large group of rowdy goats, large and small. Those goats climb all over those stack barrels there and they climb those wooden planks, but their favorite thing is hopping up onto a donkey's back, then the other, and sometimes just standing there, playing king or queen of the donkey back."

She laughed. "Not the mountain but the donkey's back."

He grinned widely. "Exactly. They are lovers of romping and jumping and playing. The donkeys chase them sometimes, and they chase the donkeys sometimes. But the majority of time, those two just stand there and the goats use them as playground equipment. It's just funny to me."

She placed her palms on her hips, grinning as she watched, not expecting what was about to happen—though he knew what was about to go down. He was surprised it hadn't already occurred. Then again, the goats weren't as little as they'd been two months ago, so they were a tad bit less aggressive. Especially when they had been in the middle of who's the king of the donkey. Now, the small adolescent goats raced toward them. Their legs were longer, and they basically galloped up. He stepped back a step so they'd get to Kelsy first and she'd get all the attention. This was her first meeting with them, so he wanted her to enjoy all of it.

As they approached, her smile widened. Her green eyes were bright as the first eight kids reached her, lifted up on their hind legs and slapped their front feet on her waist and hips. She looked as if she wore a Hawaiian grass skirt made of goats, and she was surrounded by all the others. The singing of the goats rang out.

She quickly began petting all their foreheads, was licked and nudged as she went along. She started to giggle. *Giggle.*

Startled, he chuckled. It was not exactly the sound he had envisioned coming from her but it made him smile. She was a strong woman, seemed to be anyway, and she *giggled.* He laughed, watching her. Drawn to her. "Well, I tell you, that giggle startled me."

Her giggle shifted to a hard laugh as her gaze met his. "I know. I hate it. It's been with me since I was little, and again, I hate it. But I can't help it. When something really tickles me, I giggle. I'm sorry."

"It's okay. Yeah, I was startled but I like it—" *Why had he said that?*

She yanked her gaze from him and back to the goats they called kids when young, and it fit perfectly. His attention was drawn to the door on the porch as it opened, and West and Genna came out onto the porch. They were both laughing as they came down the steps and toward them.

"It's wonderful, isn't it." Genna came up and

started to pet the kids that weren't getting to surround Kelsy so now gave their attention to her. "They like you."

Now they both had goats propped on their hips, clamoring for attention.

"I love them, adore them. They're wonderful. I'm not going to get any because my future plans are still uncertain. I wasn't sure if I'd stay with Granddad, but…I'm starting to think I will. However, I won't be getting goats, so you might be bugged to death because I want to come play so much. Or I could split it up and go to your sister-in-law Sydney and that sweet Hazel and play with theirs some." She grinned.

One of the larger mother goats had moved close and let out a long, loud maaing sound that rang out like a singing solo.

They all laughed.

Her words hadn't made him laugh, though; they struck deep. *She might be staying…*

"So you might stay," Genna gasped with excitement. "That's wonderful. And about the goats, Hazel will love it if you go out to see hers, so no problem."

"Thanks, I'll enjoy it too. Who wouldn't. And we'll see what I decide."

"They would love that and so would I, so you're welcome any time," Genna said with enthusiasm. "We would all enjoy having you stick around. And I can't wait to talk to you more about the online business I fully believe you should open."

Kelsy bit her lip as her smile spread out wide. "I'm really thinking about it. I love it here."

"Great," Genna replied. "So now that we've met all my baby goats and their mothers have been watching closely, let's all go inside and eat. Then we can sit out on the porch and talk—and play."

His sister-in-law was a great woman and he liked the way she and Kelsy seemed to get along. Then again, he hadn't met anyone who didn't like Genna. Kelsy, though younger, seemed to have that same effect. At least on him.

Once again, he slammed that thought down to the ground and tried to mentally cover it with dirt. "Sounds good to me," he said.

"Me too," Kelsy agreed.

West lifted his hand and grinned. "Then let's head inside. The house smells great since Genna made some baked sweet potatoes and fresh creamed corn she bought over at Calhoun's Feed and Seed. He's got his fresh vegetables opened up now as farmers are bringing food to supply the town through his store."

"That's a great idea," Kelsy said, "and might be where Granddad got the vegetables he had the other day that I saw sitting on the counter."

"Probably so. Bo doing that helps out everyone who doesn't have the time to grow their own. And it's all going to go great with my grilled pork I've made for everyone."

"It sounds delicious," Ace said, and they all followed his cousin through the yard, with goats romping beside them on the way to the porch.

Ace trailed behind everyone. After West held the screen door open for Genna, Ace took the door, waved him forward, and then he held it for Kelsy before he followed her in. He got a slight whiff of something sweet. He hadn't been close enough to her today to realize she wore a very light-scented perfume, bath oil, shampoo—something…and he realized he'd smelled it the night of the dance; he'd just had so much other stuff on his mind that night that he just now realized it. It was sweet. If he'd been a baby goat, he might have reached over, slung an arm around her and pulled her close. Not that the goats had done that, but that'd be the closest way of getting near her like they'd done—and been allowed to do.

*Halt!* Again, where had his brain gone?

# CHAPTER TEN

Kelsy was having a wonderful time. She really enjoyed Genna, and West also. She liked the way they got along. And as they were all sitting there at the huge dining table they said had been built by their grandfather, she glanced around at the pictures. They were everywhere and they all showed the love that the grandparents had for their two sons and families. Just like her granddad had pictures of her everywhere, so did West and Genna, left by his grandparents and carried on by them. The house was wonderful. And the pictures were, too. They were all so young and growing up, and there was one of Ace, Hunter, and their dad; it was adorable. He was probably only maybe five in the photo. But the one that stood out was the large picture that hung on the wall where the long dining table sat of all of the family before Ace and Hunter had lost their parents. It was so touching.

Again, she had the picture of her and her granddad—not the same one that her granddad had; that was the last one they'd had taken together on the fishing trip before he'd disappeared out of her life. But it was one she'd kept of all of them as a family—her beautiful grandma with her long, braided blonde hair, her cowboy hat and that smile as she leaned into her granddad, whose arm was around her as they looked into each other's happy, glowing eyes. His other arm rested on one of Kelsy's shoulders. Her parents held each other at the waist, with her father's free hand on Kelsy's other shoulder, and she was smiling like the sun on a bright,sunny day. She was so very thankful for whoever had taken the photo of the way they had been. Oh, what a time that had been when her family had been one, had been happy and oh so memorable.

It was before her grandmother's tragic death.

Before that tragedy and their responses to it had torn them apart.

Kelsy felt suddenly like she knew that was it. One

thing was for certain: she was going to push and find out whether she was right. And if she wasn't right, she was going to push so hard someone in her family finally fessed up. But looking at the happy pictures of Ace's family, the bonding of family hit her hard, and she felt as if her mind and heart had hit on something.

Something that finally made sense to her.

That was her favorite picture and she'd brought it with her, but it was still in the zipper compartment of her suitcase. That was the way she remembered her family—just like this was the picture of Ace's much larger family. She knew that the photos were wonderful. She pushed the thoughts away, realizing she was missing the conversation going on at the table.

West was laughing and looked at her. "We were talking the other day about the first time Ace and Hunter got on the Shetland ponies their dad had bought them. He hid them out here on this ranch in the stalls in the red barn. They had been so excited when Uncle Jed had led them out to the open field. One was a silver tone that shined in the sun, and the other was a light tan that drew Hunter to it instantly, as if they connected or something.

That left Ace with the silver-toned pony. Though they were only about six, they'd been taking some riding lessons from their dad on some of his regular-sized mares. So, since these were little, it was as if ole Ace here thought he had everything under control. I remember his blue-green eyes were sparkling like a blue-green hot flame as he grabbed that rein from his dad's hand—"

Ace chuckled beside her. "Yeah, little did I know."

She looked at him and knew something fun was coming. His eyes sparkled like she figured they'd done during this story.

West continued, "Yep, cowboy that he was, he slung himself up on that saddle, and the moment his tiny spurs touched that short horse as his boot slid into the stirrup—at least, that's what we've always suspected happened—that little silver spitfire of a Shetland raced forward. It began bucking and kicking, twisting and zigzagging across that pasture as it went. And there was Ace, hanging on. He looked like a bronc rider in a national championship, although he didn't have a hand thrown up in the air. No, he had both his tiny hands wrapped around that saddle horn and he just hung on."

She couldn't help the laugh that escaped her at the vision of a tough little boy hanging on tight.

West grinned at her. "Hunter's horse stood still, and he and all of us watched and hooted as their dad, my fast-running uncle, blasted across that pasture in pursuit. It is a great memory, thankfully. This fella didn't fall off; he held on till his dad got there and grabbed the trailing reins, even though the horse had started calming down, which allowed him to catch up to the them. He halted that horse and that crazy Ace behaved like he was an NFR champion rider. He threw his leg over the saddle horn and jumped from the back of that horse. He landed on his booted feet while we were hooting and laughing, and he spun toward us and across that distance his grin was huge, and he held his arms up like a champion. He knew he'd ridden that horse and he never let that moment go. Uncle Jed was grinning as he walked up and put his arm on Ace's shoulder and to this day, it's a mental photo of them I'll never lose." He chuckled. "We laugh about it often but the truth is this dude can ride a horse. And fish."

They were all laughing, and she loved it. "Well, I don't think I'll be getting on a bucking horse with him, but he is taking me fishing tomorrow. Well, not exactly fishing. We're going to look for something that might be making a stream get low."

West and Genna looked at each other, and she saw Genna's brow lift slightly before they both looked back at her.

"So you're going over on the south end of the ranch with him tomorrow to check on the water?"

"Yes." She glanced at Ace, his eyes were still bright from the laughter they'd all shared at his expense but he said nothing. "I haven't really been out anywhere and when he mentioned it at Granddad's store this morning, well, before I could stop myself, I asked him if I could go along."

Genna looked at Ace. "Oh, so you didn't ask her to go? Didn't you think she might enjoy doing something like that?"

Kelsy held back an inside laugh because she knew he wouldn't have asked her to go, and she probably shouldn't be going with him because of the way she reacted to just his nearness. But they had said they would be friends, nothing more, and her granddad had really loved that she'd asked to go. More so that Ace had agreed to take her. Friends—that was the way she was looking at this. When they'd left him this afternoon, he'd been sitting in his recliner with his heating pad on, smiling as they walked out the door. That made her happy.

"Well, I hadn't even thought about it but I had promised Lumas that I'd take her fishing and so yep, we're heading out there tomorrow. We're taking my canoe. Y'all know how much I like my canoe."

"Yeah, he likes that canoe better than he likes a wider metal fishing boat with a lot more room in it."

"My canoe can go places that a metal boat with a motor can't. And this nice little place we're going to is perfect for a canoe. Not great for a propeller. It's got deep and not so deep spots. If it's rougher and I want to go there, I'll take my kayak, especially if there is a lot of rushing water because of upstream rainstorms. But it hasn't been raining too much, so it's not kayak time. Me and my canoe can head there, and there is room for

Kelsy since she said she wanted to go. So tomorrow afternoon if we go missing, you'll know where to send the rescue crews."

Everyone laughed at that, and Genna dipped her head and gave him a look. "I've only been a member of this family for a little while and a member of the community a little longer than that, but from everything I know, you have boats and fishing under control and can come out of anything, just like you made it off that little pony."

He laughed. "Well, I didn't actually have him under control but I did stay on top of him and that's what my pride and joy came from when I lifted my hands up. I held on."

She liked his words. *I held on.* She was holding on, too. Holding on to hope that her granddad and her dad could make up whatever was between them and if at all possible, she could be there to help if need be.

Kind of like whatever was going on in Ace's head, she had a feeling that fishing helped him maneuver his way through life. Even just thinking that thought had her brain ticking, and she knew she was ready and really looking forward to going fishing with him tomorrow. She shouldn't be wanting to get close to this man; she hadn't come here with even that in her mind, so that was crazy. She had to focus on being a friend.

Friend.

*Friend.*

But there was no denying that this man drew her in all types of ways, and her curiosity was about to start winning out. She wanted to know more about what ticked in his brain, behind those gorgeous blue-green eyes of his that she found looking at her often.

~*~

They had had great fun with West and Genna last night. Now, as he drove his truck with his canoe strapped onto a trailer behind it, Kelsy sat in the passenger seat. His mind was working hard, thinking about when he'd dropped her off at her home last night. They had a good time and had actually still laughed about all the fun she'd had with Genna and the goats after dinner while he and West sat on the porch and watched them all playing as the two women talked and discussed business. Yeah, she'd had fun playing with little and big goats while she and Genna talked business. The woman knew how to have fun and do business at the same time.

He'd caught West watching him but thankfully his cousin had dove into more conversation, but not personal, and he appreciated that. But right now, as he drove, his thoughts were on when they'd arrived at her home last night. The house had been dark except for the front porch light. They'd stood there in the lamplight, the glow glistening off her soft, light hair as did those eyes—green eyes highlighted with the golden glimmer surrounding them. He'd been drawn to her like a magnet, and he'd stuffed his hands into his pockets because they'd been itching to reach out like they had been when they'd danced on Saturday night and he'd pulled her into his arms. He was getting in a bind.

He needed to be fishing today, but he needed to be fishing alone. Alone out there, getting his brain straight. Because, right now, it was kicking around inside his skull like a crazed bucking bull. He was messed up.

But oh, how he had wanted to kiss her last night.

And, for a moment, as they'd stood there last night in that porch light, staring at each other, he'd felt as if she wanted to kiss him too. But he wasn't going to get stuck on that. They were going fishing and to find out if there was something wrong with the water in his lake and the stream leading to it.

So he drove.

It was several miles to get to the south side of the ranch, almost twenty actually. They talked a little bit about the goats. Goats were a good topic to keep you off other things, and they were things you could laugh about, which helped get his mind off…other things.

And he needed that, so when she first said something about the goats, he readily joined in. Maybe a little too eagerly but he did it anyway, glad to have the distraction. Thankfully, by the time they pulled up to the stream deep in the pasture, he was more focused. And she was interested in the adventure.

"So what do you think is causing the problem? Because that doesn't look low to me." She stared out over the gently flowing water that ran right up to the edge of the land it ran through.

"This is a good area for a canoe. It's not a rapid flow from here down to the lake it empties into, so we'll put out lines and fish along the way as we check out what I'm thinking might be the problem. If it's what I think, then it will be visible somewhere along the way."

"Okay. I hope I'm not bugging you by coming, but Granddad had all those weekend fishermen who come in today. He told me how they come in and talk and talk about fishing. It sounds like a good buddy reunion, and I don't know…I just felt like I'd be intruding on them. This outing gave me a way out of hanging around and maybe being in their way. And not hurt Granddad's feelings. So, thank you."

"Gotcha, and glad to help. I'll unload the canoe and grab the poles. And there's a small cooler with some cold water. Only thing I couldn't pack is a restroom, so if you need one, I'll pull over to the bank and you can go hide behind a bush."

She laughed. "Well, believe me, I know how to do that. I fished many years as a young girl with my granddad, so it won't be a hard thing. So thanks for the offer." They both grinned; it was hard not to. "I'll just help you any way I can. Should I get the fishing poles?"

"Nope, already tied down inside, so I think we're good to go. You got your shades already on your head, your jeans tucked into your boots, your long-sleeve denim shirt—I think you must have been copying me. It protects you from too much sun." He held his arms out, showing off his boots, jeans, and denim shirt that he wore untucked on fishing days. "If you weren't shorter than me and that long, pretty blonde hair was a little darker like mine, people might think we were twins today by our outfits." He grinned. "There's enough difference in us, but we could still be considered twins." *Where was he going?* Maybe he was trying to convince himself to think of her in that way; then she was just a friend. He sighed. He was digging a hole that was going to fill up with water soon and he might drown. "Anyway, you're dressed right, and I didn't even have to tell you what to wear."

Her smile widened. "You know from that picture you saw that I had shorts on and a tank top but I was only eight and we'd been fishing on the pier. But I had an umbrella not too far away, and my mom had me covered up in sunscreen. But when me and Granddad were fishing around at home, he taught me to cover up from the sun. Protection so I don't have to worry about getting sunburned and these long-sleeved denim shirts work great."

"Exactly. I'm telling you—Lumas…that man knows his business, and you obviously listen well."

"Yes, he does. And so do you."

He liked that she thought that. Liked it more than he needed to.

~*~

"It is so lovely, a scenic view for certain." It was more of a stream than a river. It was wide but narrow in other spots, and there were beautiful trees and greenery along it and a few scatterings of flowers. He paddled and told her she could if she wanted to but that he didn't need her if she just wanted to enjoy the scenery. She'd helped for a moment but then placed her oar across her lap as she took in the beautiful scenery.

After they'd gone a little ways, he dropped an

anchor at the rear and told her to drop the one on the front. She did it, and then there they sat and fished for an hour. He'd brought her a rod similar to his, and she loved it. They were nice poles, not new.

"So," she started, after they'd been fishing for a few minutes. "Did you get these fishing rods new or from Granddad's store?"

He grinned. "You know I didn't buy it new. If I buy something, it comes from your granddad's place. I like the experience of testing out things from the past. So he saves things for me like that lure that we're supposed to test out."

She grinned at him. "You know, we have more to do than have a fishing contest with the lures. I didn't bring mine today. But listen, if we don't need to fish, we don't have to. I know you need to move on down and check out what your cousin told you about."

"We will. I just wanted to give you a little time to fish on the creek. This is one of my favorite places, and we'll end it at my favorite of all places. It has a little bit of history to it. I think you'll enjoy it."

"Okay, well, now you have me. Let's pull these in

and go forward and see if the water is lower. I don't see it here at all."

"Okay then, let's go. If what I'm expecting to find is really what's going on, we'll soon know."

They pulled their anchors and he rowed them forward.

She kept her paddle in her lap and stared out ahead for a moment, then looked back at him. "Okay, so what do you think the problem is? You obviously have a clue."

He hefted a shoulder. "I'm thinking beavers. And not far down there, I'm expecting to see the beginnings of a dam. I like beavers—they are cute little critters—but if they're building a dam, then that's not good. I dread having to move them. But if it's what I think, I'll deal with it. I don't want them blocking the water from my lake. I like riding my canoe all the way down to it. That's what we'll be checking out."

"Okay, now you have my curiosity up." She was actually thrilled that he was going to take her somewhere that he obviously really loved and she wanted to find out if he was right.

"Onward," he said, grinning as he started paddling stronger strokes. He didn't need her help but she wanted to help any way she could, and letting him get going was what she could do. And now she couldn't wait to see where he was taking her. The stream turned a large curve and then another. But as they rounded a third bend, there were two beavers sitting there in the water and behind them, where the water narrowed, she could see that they were building something. And on the land, she saw a few trees that had been gnawed. On the side of the stream, they were building a dam.

"You were right," she said over her shoulder and at the same time noticed the water near her moving quickly. And then a head of a beaver burst up and then the animal practically flew out of the water and landed, wet as a fish, on her lap! She screamed, threw her arms up, and, at the same time, because the paddle was in her lap and the beaver's feet were on it, she tossed the not-so-huge beaver back out into the water. She watched as it splashed into the water, its tail slapping as it went and sending more water her way. Gasping, she looked behind her.

Ace was cracking up.

"He dove in here. He just came up out of the water like a torpedo blasting up through the surface."

"Yeah, it was terrible but I'm sorry—your reaction was why I'm laughing. You did good and got rid of him before he could hurt you. I would have been there to help you but your great reaction took care of it. I'm so sorry. I didn't expect that to happen or want it to happen." He chuckled. "But you had it under control. You slung him up in the air, and he dove back in like he was an Olympic champion diver. And there he is again."

She spun from looking at Ace and spotted the beaver coming back her way. "What is he doing?"

"He's protecting the dam that he's building, the habitat that he's creating in doing so."

"What do I do?" Her voice rang out in an excited uproar. *Maybe he's going to jump in the middle of the boat.*

"Hold that paddle out in front of you. He's just going to come up here and gripe at us. Basically telling us that this is his place."

That was exactly what the little critter did: it

stopped just a few feet from them and proceeded to tell them in his language that he wanted them to leave. *Go. Now*, she could almost hear the beaver rattling off in beaver language.

As he was doing that, Ace took his oar and pushed them forward so they headed toward the opening that was to the side of the new dam that was being built, more to the side of the water and across it. Thankfully there was room for them and it wasn't clogged up completely. They went through and continued on. And no beaver followed them. It was clear that the water was lower as they entered this area.

"Your cousin actually saw it was lower?"

"Yep, that fella knew something was up. But it's going to be okay."

"It is?" She continued looking over her shoulder at the amazing man.

"Yep. They're not building it across the stream but the side. It'll stop the water some and divert it to the land behind their dam. This will make a new habitat for that area but my lake up ahead will be okay. For this piece of land, it's going to be fine. At least for now. And you're okay—it didn't bite you or slap you with that paddle called his tail."

She smiled. "Well, I have to say that it was an adventure and that I'm glad it didn't slap me in the face with its flat paddle tail or bite me." She laughed, and he laughed too, and the sound sent joy racing through her. She stared at him. *Oh my goodness.* Her heart did a flip, a flip like the beaver had done back into the water. In that moment, she knew she was in trouble.

She turned back around and watched the water ahead of her as she pondered what had just slammed into her.

# CHAPTER ELEVEN

Ace had known this was going to be tough. Something about this woman did things to him that no one else had ever done before. But because his buddy Lumas had asked him to help, here he was, about to take her to his favorite place—the place he'd come with his dad many times before he died. The lake on the south had a beautiful stone pier overhanging the small lake; it flowed because of the stream spilling into it and then moved on through the smaller outlet on the far side of the lake. He'd been worried about the beavers messing up the flow but had relief about that now, and the only thing on his mind was Kelsy.

She had turned away from him and said little after their good laughing time moments ago. It was as if maybe, for her, reality had slammed into her the way it had him. He didn't push more conversation and she didn't either, but he had brought her here. "So, that up there is the lake. It has a pier that I think you'll like. See—it's there across the way, now that we are officially on the lake. This land wasn't part of the original ranch but when all the oil money started coming in, this is some of the first land Granddad bought with the money. There is an old church back behind the pier that collapsed before we bought the land, and some old headstones from an old graveyard. We assume there must have been some people ages ago who settled here. So we leave it alone but I find peace here. I think you're going to like standing there on that stone pier those folks from so long ago must have built. I used to fish off that pier and also canoe here with my dad. This was our special spot. Hunter didn't like fishing much, but horses were his thing. So, him and Dad had their horse events, and me and Dad fished. Hunter and I have many memories that are different because our interests aren't always the same." He smiled. "Just because we're twins, it doesn't mean we're exactly alike. We have several different things we favor; fishing was my joy with my dad, and this place is where the joys are greatest."

She had turned and was looking at him again as he headed the canoe across the wide lake. "I," her voice wavered, "I can tell it's very important to you here. And now, knowing how important it is to you…oh Ace, thank you for bringing me. I can't wait to fish from the pier you and your dad loved so much. Is that what you think about when you step out on it? About the joy you had with your dad? That's my main thoughts, my time with my granddad. You and I have that in common. Fishing was—is still for me, thank the good Lord—but it is the thing we share. I feel so bad for you. I know that the way you feel is the way I was feeling, but the fact that you brought me here to this special place and the fact that the sneaky beavers allowed me the opportunity to come—I'm so sorry if it was only because I asked if I could come with you. I know you didn't offer in the first place. You were just so nice and instead of turning me down, you brought me. And I can't tell you…" Her voice trembled as she stared at him, and his heart did the same.

He had never brought anyone here. His brother and

cousins came when they were herding cattle but as far as he knew, no one else fished in this lake or canoed in the stream. But he'd let her come.

~*~

Kelsy realized how important this place was to him. He and his dad's special place, and here she was. She tried not to make more out of it than it was, but right now she wasn't going away. Because he had brought her here and because of that, he deserved to know how much it touched her. He was staring at her and at the same time directing the canoe toward the land.

"The one thing I can say is I've never brought anyone here before and never planned on it, because I really didn't think about it much. But, the deal is, of all people who would understand, it's you. So I don't feel bad that I brought you here."

Her heart pounded. She had said what she felt and meant it. He had brought her here even after he hadn't invited her to his private place; because of her grandad, he'd brought her to this wonderful, amazing place that was so cherished by him. And for that she was thankful because it opened up a deep connection to him. And as much as she was trying to look at what had so quickly grown between them as friendship, she knew, for her, though she hadn't been looking for it, she could care for this amazing man like she had never cared for anyone. They had so many things in common…but looking at him now, she had to get her mind off all of that.

They had found the beavers making themselves a home, and he was fine with it, okay with the beavers making a habitat on his special area. And until now, she hadn't realized how important this area was to him. Now she knew. And she needed to back away. She had to make sure this wonderful fella had a good time and didn't regret bringing her on this trip. She was going to fish and not go into anything more that he might not want her digging into. But obviously this was his spot. The place he came for time alone. He fished all over, evidently, but this spot was his special place.

He came here to fish, to remember his dad and…hide?

"Okay, are we going to fish now?" she asked as

they reached the shore. He stepped out in his rubber boots and stood still in the water, holding the canoe still as she stepped onto the grass.

"Yep, I'm happy the beavers will be able to stay and now we're going to fish."

She smiled at him. Her brain was churning but right now they were going to fish and enjoy themselves. And build that "friendship" that they were building.

Within moments, they were out on the pier. He and she had brought their poles and were casting out into the calm water.

He smiled over at her. "Peaceful?"

Oh, it was. "Yes, unbelievably so. Ace, it's amazing. I think I could stand here all day. And even the birds are about as happy as they could be on this beautiful day." Her gaze had lifted to the birds gliding above them on their black wings.

"Yes. You do know those are buzzards." He grinned.

"Hey, yes I know they're buzzards, but they're floating along and loving it. Just like they make the sky more beautiful with their flight. And when they're not gliding, they're cleaning up everything. Farmers, ranchers, and even people out on the highways, would have big messes to clean up if there weren't those graceful flying birds. They know how to clean up and do their jobs well."

He grinned as he reeled his line in. "I laugh at that because I remember when I was…about five. I remember me and Dad were standing out here on this pier and I made a similar statement like that. Dad said, 'Yep, they're pretty up in the sky but when they're down here on the ground, they're nasty. Don't go up to them when they're eating because all they eat are dead things.' I laughed; I thought that was funny that that was what they did. But that was before I knew that God had known what He was doing when He gave us birds that knew how to clean up things. Anyway, I was a kid, and kids find the oddest things funny."

She smiled. "I have to say, I never really thought about it, but at five, I can see how you thought that was funny."

"Yeah, but then I thought about it, and I looked up at them and yelled, 'Don't come eat my fish.' Dad laughed at that. I was always thinking about my fish. Memories are good, aren't they?"

"Yes, they are. I lost my granddad when I was eight, and decided that he was dead and all of his memory was…" She paused, not wanting to go there.

"And what?"

She met his gaze.

"What is it about it that you didn't understand? Why didn't your dad tell you that your granddad wasn't dead?"

"I don't know. He didn't tell me he was dead, but I didn't ask. My dad lost his mother. And he loves bucking bulls. He loved it when he rode them, competed on them, and has a wall full of metal belt buckles from his wins through all his years of riding. Then so many of the bulls he raises have won awards that he also has on the wall—pictures of his top-ranked bulls are everywhere. He also has pictures of my grandma running barrels in the many top competitions she competed in and won many times. She really could ride. She didn't always make it into the National Finals Rodeo, but she did many times. My dad has photos of her wins, her smiling, beautiful face along with her beloved horses. One of the things I noticed when I entered Granddad's home is there are no pictures of her barrel racing on her horses or smiling at the camera after she'd won. There are pictures of her smiling with all of us, but there is not one picture of her in that house of her on a horse, standing still or racing around a barrel.

"I think when that bull killed her, it was just such a totally crazy thing. She was in the back and the bull got loose somehow and it found her. And before anyone could get in and pull her out of that enclosure, she was gone. She had won that night. And they lost her that night. And, well, I was seven at the time and even then my granddad was so sad. He wasn't himself. I tried to love on him, but he didn't come to our house much.

"We had a fishing trip planned that Grandma was supposed to go on with us in Marathon, Florida. So we went, but even me, at the young age I was, knew something wasn't right, so I spent every moment I could with Granddad. We fished off the pier and in a small boat out in the bay, but Dad and Granddad didn't fish together on that trip. And now, as I've been thinking about it, I realized that if Dad was outside, Granddad was in the house or taking me for a walk to play on the playground in the neighborhood. Along the way, there were beautiful trees with red blooms. I learned they're royal poinciana trees. I loved them.

"Anyway, we had a small boat and then the bigger rented boat. I went with Mom and Dad a few times on the rented boat, but Granddad didn't go. He went out in the small boat to fish in the bay, so, after that, I spent the last three days fishing with him in the little boat or on the pier. That picture of me and him that he has in his office was the last picture we took. Mom and Dad got back, and I showed her the fish; she used Granddad's camera for that photo. As you can tell, the sun was going down, so Mom took me in and got me ready for bed and I went to sleep. The next day, everything changed."

~*~


Ace had known something had happened, and now he completely understood. Lumas had lost his love like he'd told him, and he and his son obviously couldn't agree on how to mourn her loss. He had no pictures of her rodeo days, not wanting to remember her barrel racing. He had no pictures of that. Never mentioned it. And he had obviously that night they'd been at such a disagreement over it that he left? "So, the next morning, your granddad left."

She wound her line in and then laid her pole on the pier and then nodded. "Yes. He was packed when I woke up, and he hugged me. My mom was leaning against the counter in the kitchen with a cup of coffee in her hands, saying nothing. I could understand she didn't know how to handle it. I've thought about it, and because she loved my dad, I think she kept her thoughts to herself. I understand that, to a point. But he hugged me and told me he had to go and that he would see me later. And I never saw him again. Until I came here, that is."

Tears glistened in her eyes, and his heart ached.

"I asked about him and for the first little while when I asked where Granddad was, they'd just tell me that he couldn't make it. And as I grew up, I had a friend who lost her granddad. He died and she hurt like I was hurting, and she was always bothered like me because she never saw him anymore. So, in my mind, I assumed he died too, and they didn't want to tell me. I was so wrong.

"Two months ago, I was up in Mom and Dad's attic, looking for things to donate to a bookstore, I forgot that, but as I was digging through a box on the bottom shelf, a box from the top shelf fell down…the top flew off and a mass of envelopes—a red one, a blue one, green…all colors—scattered across the floor. And they all had my name on them. I sank to the floor and opened one. It was a birthday card to me from Granddad. The next one was a Christmas card. And an Easter card. Lots and lots of cards. He'd write notes, telling me he loved me and missed me and sorry we weren't getting to see each other. But that one day, if I wanted to know where he was, I was now old enough to know, so he gave me his address and told me I was welcome any time. The date of the card was my eighteenth birthday. And the cards had continued. I got one this year. I'm a March birthday girl, the ninth, and it was in there among all those that were piled up around me when I sat on the floor and cried. He knew that by then I could make choices for myself. He must have assumed I was getting the cards and just wasn't answering him."

"This is terrible. Have you talked about it with him?"

"No. We are just so glad to be together again that neither of us has opened up the topic. Yes, he knows Dad never gave me the cards. But we didn't go any deeper than that. I think he and I both don't want anything to interrupt how good it feels to be together again."

Ace had stopped fishing during her stunning story. He reeled his line in and laid it on the ground, hearing the tremble of her words and feeling them dig deep into his heart. His thoughts whirled as he looked into those amazing sad eyes of hers; then he took a step toward her and embraced her. Pulled her close to his heart. It was as if they were on the dance floor again, but this time tears from her eyes wetted his shirt as she leaned her head on him and cried.

And Ace's heart broke for her. His mom and dad *had* died, and he'd lost them. But he'd known what happened to them, and he'd known that everything between his mom and dad and everyone was all good. There was no family problem that ran deep like this and tore them apart. As he held her and let her cry, let her tears fall there right above his heart, his heart opened wide. She'd had to endure all of this, knowing something had happened and not knowing what. She'd lost a grandmother, then a granddad—or at least thought she had because no one had told her the truth. Anger, even anger at Lumas, twisted inside him. She'd had to create in her own young mind an excuse of why he'd not come around, so she'd believed he'd died. And her dad and mother had let her believe that. Believe what she wanted so they didn't have to talk about it. They'd hidden the truth from her.

He had the urge to kiss the top of her head but didn't. Instead, he fought to give reason to her reactions. "If I was in your shoes, I'd be really upset too. But, you know, the death of loved ones affects everyone differently. The one thing you can be sure of is your grandmother was loved. Greatly. Each one of your loved ones loved her and had their own way of dealing with her death—their loss of her, their mourning her loss. I can only imagine that she's in heaven, looking down and hoping that something helps her son and daughter-in-law and her husband get over her loss. Get over their differences and understand that they all loved her in their own way and couldn't let her go." His voice trembled with the emotion he felt, how he knew this and how he hoped he could help her.

"I loved my mom and dad, and I'll just be honest with you. Dancing was what I did with my mom. My mom could dance. She loved it, and she and Dad fell in love on the dance floor. I can remember her telling me that. She knew the night they had their second dance that there was something different between them than anyone else she'd ever danced with. She said the first time she danced with him, she really was drawn to him. He was a good dancer, not the best though—she'd danced with some of the best." He smiled, remembering. "She was a great dancer and felt it was her duty to teach me and Hunter to dance. And so, he and I both danced but…well, we deal with grief in different ways. He dances a lot and me, not so much."

She looked up at him and wiped her eyes with the fingers of her left hand. Her right hand was pressed hard against his back, and he felt it as if it were reaching through him and taking hold of his heart since it was on that side of his body.

"Yes, we do handle grief in different ways. And Ace, thank you, because you have shown me something today. My grandma, oh goodness, I loved her like you loved your mom and dad. And I lost her. But now, I get it. That day I was up there in that attic, looking for books to donate, I don't know what knocked that box off that shelf. It was a sturdy shelf tightly connected to the wall. But suddenly, I think—I don't particularly believe in ghosts, but I know my grandma is up in heaven and she could have willed that box to fall. Miracles do happen, and I now understand. You had it right. I am the one who is supposed to get my granddad and my dad and mom back together again." Tears swept down her face. "It's very clear to me now," she ground out through clenched teeth, trying to hold her emotions back so the words could be understood. "And you." She smiled. "You wonderful man, I'll always cherish this day because you helped me see what I'm supposed to do."

And then she slid her hand from his back up to his neck and lifted up on her tiptoes; his head was already leaned down as he looked into her eyes. But now she cupped her hand around his nape, tugged him closer, and kissed him.

# CHAPTER TWELVE

Kelsy had such emotions flowing through her that she had spontaneously reached up to give this wonderful man a kiss of thanks, of gratitude. A quick kiss—just a quick kiss—but his lips had sent a huge shocking sense of vibrant emotion flooding through her. She felt grateful for understanding her place in her father's and granddad's lives when she'd kissed him. But now, as every thought in her mind muddled and all she could feel was him, his lips, his arms and heart holding her close, she couldn't let go. She…felt so deeply connected. So…she couldn't do this.

She knew what she was supposed to do now; she could not let herself fall for this wonderful, amazing man who had helped her by telling her something that he'd never told anyone. But he was kissing her. Their lips melded together; his arms tightened around her, and it felt as though they were one. But, he would regret this. She knew he would. He had clearly said he wasn't looking for this, and she got it now. She didn't want to, but she was a strong person so she pushed away, her lips aching to go back as she looked up into his eyes. They looked stunned and so bright, so bright blue-green, but more blue than usual—as if he floated in clouds. *Oh what a thought that was, but no. No, no, no.* "I'm sorry. I got a little overexcited. But thank you. I will always be grateful to you. And now, we should go. I have to figure out how to deal with this. How to get Mom and Dad and Granddad together. And I think…I might have to go back home. Anyway, I don't really know, I'm still thinking." She forced herself to step back from him, as badly as she hated it, and he let go of her, still having said nothing. "Ace, can you take me back?"

"Yes, I can do that." He reached down, picked up their rods, and they headed toward the canoe.

She stopped. "Oh, I wasn't thinking. We have to go all the way back in the canoe." As beautiful as it had been, it would be a long ride back now.

"No. We just have to carry it down that trail right there. I have an old Jeep that I use when I don't have time or want to go all the way back in the boat, back to my truck. We'll ride it to the truck and then the next time I come fishing, I'll start from this end and drive it back here to my truck. So you carry the rods," he handed them to her, "and I'll strap the drink bag on my back, and we'll head that way."

There was no emotion in his words, not anything about the kiss. Then he strapped the bag across his shoulder, lifted the canoe, topped it over above his head, and started to walk.

And she followed him.

"Granddad, I need to talk to you," Kelsy said later that evening after Ace had brought her home and she'd waited for her granddad to come home from work. "I enjoyed my afternoon with Ace. But something happened, a realization came to me while we were out there looking for those beavers. That's what it turned out to be, beavers. They were building a lodge but thankfully they were building it to the side, not across the stream that supplies water to his lake. But, he will have another water area that will fill up around the low-lying tree area that will give life to another group of animals and birds. And to be honest, I loved Ace's reaction to finding them. He wasn't worried about it. He said that that land was bought after all that oil was discovered on their land. I didn't even know they were all so wealthy. The man doesn't even act like he has all of that.

"He loves ranching and fishing, and Granddad, I'm not going to say everything we talked about because I don't have the right, but I'm going to tell you what I discovered while we were looking for the beavers. I need to make sure that you and Dad make up. Like Ace came to a compromise, an understanding that those beavers can live there, and he can still have his lake. They can make a compromise, and it'll be good for both him and the beavers. He has wonderful memories there on that beautiful lake of him and his dad. He loved being there fishing, just him and his dad. His dad, who he lost and knows he won't ever see again until he reaches heaven and they reunite.

"But Granddad, you and my dad have to come to an agreement, or at least a compromise like Ace did with the beavers. I've really thought about this. Thought about it from the moment the realization hit me of what happened. See, all these years, I thought you were dead, and my dad didn't straighten me out on that. I never actually said that I thought you were dead, but he never actually said why he never told me the truth. You never called and explained and since we've never talked about it, it was finding all of your cards that you sent me all these years that I never got from Dad. I'm sure it was Dad and not Mom because she never said anything, just supported Dad, and I think it bothers her. I'll talk to her about it but I feel like this is between you and Dad, and it is because of Grandma. Isn't it?"

Her granddad stared at her as if she had opened a jar of sour pickles and thrown them at him. But she didn't back down. She knew this was what she was supposed to do. Whether she did it right or not, she just hoped that she had the ability to get through to them, because oh yes, she was going to talk to her dad too.

"Darlin', I left and yes, your dad and I disagreed on how to handle things after your grandmother died. I held deep resentment for the rodeo. Yes, your grandma loved her rodeoing but just looking around and seeing all of those pictures of her and the knowledge that it took her away from me, I couldn't take it. And your dad insisted on keeping all those pictures up of her, and he continued to ride bulls and raise those horrible bulls like the one that had killed your grandmother. And on that fishing trip, I couldn't take it anymore."

He met her gaze and Kelsy's heart clenched. "So, you left."

He nodded. "I packed up, put my house on the market, and drove. I had no idea where I was going. Your dad didn't care, and as much as it hurt my heart to leave you, I also knew it wasn't my right to come between you and your dad. I love you with all my heart, sweetie…" His words trembled and his big eyes welled with tears.

Kelsy reached out and placed her hand on his arm. "I know."

"But I couldn't deal with everything. Your grandma loved you too, and she loved rodeoing, but I couldn't deal with that anymore. I have tried through the years to get my brain to wrap around that. And, honestly, you coming here and not pressuring me, and me seeing how beautiful you have turned out in your heart and your mind and yourself, you remind me so much of your grandmother. I've missed you, and I've missed your mom and…I've missed your dad. And I've missed your grandma. And you coming here, confronting me like this…" He wiped tears off his cheek and smiled at her. "Your grandma would have done exactly that. Believe me, that strong-willed cowgirl would have set me straight early on. And she's tried in my brain and my dreams, and I've ignored her. I should have known something was wrong when I never heard a word from you after you were old enough to contact me. But in my heart of hearts, I wasn't ready."

Her heart ached but his words sent a jolt of hope through her. "Do you think that you could ever embrace my dad again? Maybe be okay that he mourns Grandma and yet he honors what she loved? He is so proud of her achievements. He told me all the time what a great person she was, what a champion rodeo rider she was. He loved that. And he told me that just because they had an accident in that arena and that bull got out, that she wouldn't have held it against the bull. That it was just doing what it was trained for. And I didn't know all of this until now, when I put everything together, but I know Grandma did. And you knew her, too, and you've been hearing her words, her hopes, and I can guarantee you that when I ask Dad—if she's talking to you and she's talking with me, I have a feeling she's been talking to Dad too…maybe not in words but through her love.

"He knows I'm here. I left him a note that told him now that I knew you were alive, I was coming to see you. And I was going to find out why no one told me you were alive and what had happened. I told him I was really angry—no, he never told me you were dead but he knew that was what I believed and he never said otherwise. In my small, young mind, because they never talked about you and you never came around, that's what I believed. My friend's granddad died and she never heard from him or saw him, so in my heart, that's what I had to believe, that the man I loved so much hadn't just left me. But that he'd died and couldn't contact me.

"And then that day in the attic, that box of cards fell off that shelf and today when I was out there on that stream with Ace, I realized that I think Grandma had something to do with those cards falling off that shelf. I'm old enough to deal with things, and it was time for me to step in. And that is what I'm doing. Granddad, Grandma would not want you and Dad living a life separated like this. And I think she was telling me to make sure you two make up. And don't destroy your love and life together because of her. She doesn't deserve that. She loved both of y'all and she would want both of y'all together, not to be separated because of her."

Her voice shook with tears but she carried on. "You can't control how he remembers, and he can't control the same for you. But y'all can control how you honor each other's love for her by showing your love to each other. Like she would or is wanting you to. And I know that is why she helped me stand here right now. I'm not backing away from what I believe is my destiny in bringing the two men I love back together. That's what she would want me to do. So, what are you going to do, Granddad?"

~*~

Lumas's heart was ripped apart by his sweet granddaughter's words. By the look on her face, the anguish and determination in her voice, and the fact that she reminded him so much of the woman he'd lost, missed, and couldn't forget. The woman, his Dana, who he knew was looking at him right now through the eyes of the little girl they'd loved together before she'd died that night.

"Kelsy, I feel everything you've stated. And I can see in your face and your voice your grandmother talking to me. I have some thinking to do. I'm not saying no; I just need to think about this. So, tomorrow is Saturday, and I don't think I'm going to work tomorrow, so could you open the store for me?"

"I can do it. But I have to tell you that I might be

going home. It's not just you I'm supposed to talk to; it's Dad, too. That's what Grandma's urging me to do. And it's not just that I feel urging from Grandma—I feel that it's time for me to talk to my dad." Her level eyes drilled into him, and he nodded.

"You must do what you feel like you must do. And I hope that you come back. You don't have to open the store tomorrow. It can just be closed down."

"No, you listened to me and you're going to think about it, so if I'm going home, I'll go Sunday."

"Very well. I just need some time away. But now I'm going to bed. And darlin', don't ever let what I've done cause you problems. I hope what happened with you and Ace out there today, because of me, didn't cause any problems with y'alls friendship."

She closed her eyes for a moment, shook her head, then looked at him. "No, we're still friends. But he knows I'm going home to see Dad."

Lumas nodded and then headed toward the bedroom. He needed to be alone. He'd probably go fishing tomorrow. The only place he could ever really think.

By early morning, he hadn't slept but just a little, so right before daybreak he walked out to his truck, put his fishing poles and tackle box down in the back, and then he drove away. He wasn't sure where exactly he was going to go fishing but he'd find a place. Maybe someplace new. Maybe that was what he needed in his life—new things. But he didn't always dwell on his past and like his granddaughter said, it was time to talk to his son. But he had to be strong enough and he had to not say the wrong thing.

He drove down one road then another, his brain whirling with thoughts as the early morning light slowly lightened the sky. Fishing was exactly what he was thinking about. He'd just had to get out. He topped a small hill; the sun had risen just enough that at the top of the hill, it blinded him momentarily. He shut his eyes and raked a hand down his face; in that same moment, his truck smashed into something. He bumped over it, slammed on his brakes, and halted there in the middle of the road.

Behind him, he saw a good-sized branch in the middle of the road. On the side of the road, standing there staring at him, was Millie Watts. The woman held her mouth open in shock, as if he were an idiot for not seeing that branch in the middle of the road. Then his gaze went to her truck sitting there on the side of the road with a pile of wood in the back end of it. She had obviously been about to pick up the lost limb that had probably fallen off her truck.

He pressed the gas, drove off the road, then slammed the brakes, shoved it in park and practically kicked the stubborn driver's door open as he got out. "Are you okay?" he yelled, his heart pounding.

"I'm fine, not that I would have been if I hadn't been watching because I knew that sunshine was a blinder so I was being careful, even if there is hardly ever any traffic on this road. So how are you?"

He stared at her, his heart still pounding in his chest at knowing he could have run over her. He couldn't talk for a minute and took a deep breath. "I'm glad you're safe."

"Well, I tend to take care of myself and that includes watching out for sun-blinded drivers when I have not tied down the stuff in my truck bed."

"None of this was your fault. You were just picking up what you lost, and I wasn't paying enough attention. My mind was kind of muddled. It was somewhere else."

She stared at him. This woman was a beautiful woman; he had avoided her over the years since she'd moved to town, and he knew why. He never talked about what had happened to his wife but everyone knew what had happened to Millie's husband. And they had both died in similar ways. It wasn't something you'd want to talk about. So he hadn't wanted anyone to know. When he had told Ace those facts while trying to get ready for Kelsy if she needed it, he hadn't faced the fact that he needed help.

Standing there now, looking at this woman, who he knew had lost her love to a bull, brought up a lot of things he thought were way too familiar. She had loved rodeo and barrel racing just as much as his wife. And she'd been just as good. And whether she knew it or not, she and his Dana might have competed against each other. He hadn't gone and looked. It had been a long time, but he did know that when she was around that he tended to watch her. He tried not to let it be noticeable.

She had lost the man that she'd loved, and she made it very clear to everyone that she'd lost the man she loved and that was it for her. That she might be beautiful, might be a draw to the men around her age—older or younger—but she wasn't looking for anything. And as strange as that felt to him, as he looked at her, he knew he was attracted to her.

But he knew that it was because in so many ways she reminded him of his Dana, his sweet wife...the woman he'd loved with all of his heart. The woman he couldn't or didn't want to forget. And he knew that was the only way he felt attracted to this woman. They had too much in common, and he wasn't looking for anything ever again. The one thing he would never do was risk losing someone again.

Especially someone he was pretty positive drew his attention because they had so much in common with the loss of the ones they loved. And she also had loved rodeo like his sweet Dana.

# CHAPTER THIRTEEN

Millie took a deep breath as she looked at the visually distraught Lumas Camry. The man she knew had been in denial all these years. She knew who his wife was, and he'd never told anyone who he'd been married to. She'd asked a few questions early on, without anyone understanding what she was doing and quickly realized no one knew who his wife was, nobody in this town knew what an amazing cowgirl she'd been. Or that she'd been killed in a completely crazy way, just a freak accident when a bull had gotten away and she'd been in the wrong place at the wrong time. Millie had kept all of that to herself all these years. That was his business, and she understood people's business. She had loved her cowboy, bull rider that he was, and she had never forgotten how much joy she'd felt and gotten from rodeoing. She wore her boots and her winning belt buckles; she talked about it with anyone who wanted her to talk to them about it. She just hadn't ever gone back to the rodeo.

It wasn't the same without her Hank. It wasn't because she despised it or hated the bull that had killed him. It just wasn't the same.

"Could you pick that up for me, please?"

He nodded and looked both ways to make sure no one else was coming over that hill. He picked it up and headed her way. He laid it in the back of her truck with the other stuff.

She looked at him. "I know you are probably going to work but I was carrying these down to the stream that comes out down beside this road, runs along beside it then turns away and heads back into the woods. It's a good fishing hole, and I thought after picking them up from my yard that they'd be a good hiding place for some fish to challenge fishermen. Would you like to drive down there and help me?"

He looked at the truck then back at her. "Sure. I was actually going fishing this morning and maybe that's where I should go fishing."

She smiled at him, felt like she needed to encourage him—something was wrong. She could see it in his eyes. His granddaughter was in town, and she was a lovely young woman. She wondered whether something had happened between them. None of her business, but right now she just had to do what she felt was right and that was to keep him from having a wreck while his brain was obviously not where it needed to be. "Well, I'll tell you what, I'll lead the way and you just follow me." That would be the safest way of doing this. Hopefully he wouldn't pull out in front of anyone or run over something else he didn't need to run over.

"Okay, I'll do that." Without saying anything else, he turned and headed back to his truck.

She looked both ways, then pulled onto the completely deserted road. This was a highly unused road. Another reason why the fishing was good in the spot they were heading towards. She drove along and glanced in her rearview a few times, and he looked good. Maybe whatever had been on his mind had been shocked out of him when he ran over that log and he was alert again. She knew what not being alert meant. After losingHank, she hadn't been all there. Oh, she'd come home; she hadn't traveled. She'd gone to a grocery store before she'd reached town and had bought all kinds of things, and then she'd gone into the house and hadn't come out for at least a month.

As she rounded the curve, she saw where the stream curved toward the road. She drove along the road as the stream did too, and then the stream took a turn the opposite way. She slowed down, pulled onto the grass, and drove carefully through the grass, making sure it was still hard like it was supposed to be. And then she parked and got out.

Lumas did the same, and there they stood. It was a peaceful area. The grass was about knee high, but she had her boots on and her jeans tucked in. Lumas had on his rubber boots; he was ready to fish. She walked through the weeds and let down her tailgate. "So you think this is a good idea?"

He came to stand beside her. "Yeah, I do. I come fishing out here sometimes but today my brain wasn't exactly where it was supposed to be. You live farther back in the other direction, right?"

"Yes, I do. And like you said, there aren't a lot of people who come down this road. Except guys like you who know the stream has fish. Or some who come for good quiet time." She stared at him and that, she was pretty sure, was what he'd really been looking for.

He swept his fishing hat off his head—he wasn't wearing a cowboy hat. No, this was a pale-blue hat that had fishing lures hooked on it in places, and he often wore it or a similar one, she'd noticed.

"Yeah. I guess you don't ever have a day when your brain is somewhere else?"

She laughed, picked up a couple of long, not too heavy sticks, and grinned at him. "Believe me, I've had that happen a lot of days. I've had days when I knew getting behind the wheel of a vehicle was not where I needed to be."

"Yeah, I know. I get it. I deserved that."

"I wasn't being rude. I'm just saying that's how I was. Maybe you didn't realize that. I know people run over all kinds of things."

He sighed. "No, you're right. I should have been

paying better attention. I could have hurt someone. But I wasn't."

She started to walk down through the grass and he followed, carrying a couple of larger limbs. She reached the water's edge and looked out over the stream. It was pretty and flowing downstream at a slow pace, making this a nice, relaxing area. She had come here a lot after she'd lost her sweetheart; she'd sat here among the grass and a few bluebonnets that were scattered about and cry.

Now she threw the stick in her right hand out over the water. It didn't go too far because it was heavier than she'd realized it was to throw with one arm. It sank quickly; then she held the other one with both hands, dropped it to her knees, then swung it forward out over the water and watched it glide through the air and plop into the water a little farther out than the first one.

She looked over at Lumas, who stood not far from her. "I'm not as strong as I used to be but you know, I didn't need to throw them all the way across anyway."

To her surprise, he chuckled and those sad blue-gray eyes of his sparkled. Her heart had a warm, happy feeling, seeing that she'd helped bring that look back into them.

"I think you did great. I'll throw mine out there, then I guess we'll get some more and walk a little farther downstream before throwing them out? Is that what you want to do?"

"You've got the idea. I don't want to pile them all in one spot. I want them to sink down and make a habitat for the fish, but I don't want to cause a problem for the few boats that might roam around out here every once in a while."

"That's a smart idea. I wouldn't want to get my propeller caught in a bunch of wood stacked too high."

She watched as he easily tossed one stick with one hand, past the one she'd tossed with both her hands. And the second limb followed. The man was a tall, broad-shouldered muscular man, even at his mid to late sixties. But then again, she was a tall, fairly in-shape woman in her mid-fifties. She knew that didn't happen by accident. She might not ride horses anymore, but she hiked up and down trails on her land, up hills along creeks and the river that ran through her place. The ones she'd already filled with enough limbs. The place she knew there was good fishing to be had but no one ever asked to come out and she never made the offer.

She enjoyed her time exercising, other than working in her shop in town and seeing customers who came inside. And now that they were doing the dances and she was helping decorate the streets once a month, she was seeing people more than she used to. Used to be it was her shop, saying hi to a few ladies, then going home and spending the weekend alone hiking. But now she was out a little bit more, and she had to admit that she was enjoying it.

This man, on the other hand, he stayed in his shop. She had a view of his store from her front window, which was on Main Street but faced the incoming street where his store was. Sometimes, without even realizing it, she'd find herself staring out the front window and watching his store and noticing he hardly ever left, other than to dine a few times at the Mulberry Diner or just to get in his truck and drive away. This was what he did; he fished when he wasn't in his store.

"So are you doing okay?" Why she'd asked him that, she didn't know. She wasn't one to get into people's business.

"Well, I'm trying. I'm having to…" He paused, put his large hands on his hips, and stared out over the water. He had a frown on his face as he watched the water easing by. "I need to face something. I need to come to terms with a few things in my life and, well, sorry, I don't normally talk to people about that."

"Hey, I'm not much of a talker myself. But the way I look at it, maybe I was on that road today for a reason. Maybe you need someone to talk to. And my ears are open, and I'm in no hurry. But only if you want to talk or need to."

He met her gaze, and she suddenly wanted him to trust her. She didn't need anybody. Nobody—no man— had needed her for a long time but in that moment, she had a memory of how it used to be between her and Hank. And before she could even stop herself, she said it. "Does this have anything to do with your wife you lost to a bull?"

His expression was startled as their gazes locked— those words had come out before she could stop them. Now, looking at him, she knew she had hit the nail on the head.

"You know about my wife?"

She cocked her head to the side and prayed she didn't mess up. "Yes. I didn't really know her but she was someone I looked up to. There wasn't a lot of difference in our age but we traveled in different directions most of the time. I watched her, though, and know what happened to her, but I never said anything."

"No, you didn't. I had no idea. I knew about your career but I never said anything either. I never talked to anyone about Dana."

"I noticed. When I came back and you were living here and I realized who you were, I would have said something. I would have told you that I had met her a few times and how much I respected and admired her abilities. But then I realized that you had moved here and no one knew who your wife was. I figured you had a reason for that, so I kept my mouth shut."

He pulled his hat off and slapped it against his leg. Obviously the lures that were in it had protectors on the hooks or were padded with the folding that they didn't stick him. He looked back out across the water. "My life was in turmoil when I moved here. I didn't tell anyone and nobody knew it. Everybody was kind of aware that I didn't talk about my past and they didn't ask questions unless it was about fishing. And I never really thought anyone might know and just didn't say anything. But now, things are different. Yeah, I lost my wife to that crazy bull that shouldn't have been where it was and it took her out. And I've never been able to forgive it or walk away from it.

"I moved here when my son and I couldn't agree on things that had to do with her, and how we mourned her loss. I didn't want people here looking at me and feeling bad for me or talking to me about it, so I didn't say anything. I guess when I shut the door on life without my son and her and my little granddaughter, I just locked it. Now I'm standing here, and I have to face it."

"So, I mean, first, I feel bad for you. I kind of can understand. We've been through almost the same thing. It's very obvious you loved your wife and I loved my sweetie, but everybody knows when your granddaughter came to town, you were surprised and glad. So, did she not know about you? Did she not know you lived here?"

"Obviously not. I chose to leave when she was eight. As I said, her dad and I mourned differently. He, by celebrating her choices, her awards, while I despised them, hated everything he celebrated. I couldn't deal with it, and we couldn't agree, and it was getting really bad…so after the last fight, I left. I gave my darling Kelsy a hug and then drove away and I never saw her again until she showed up here the day of the last town dance. We hadn't talked about it until yesterday. She confronted me. Told me she was speaking for her grandmother."

His voice disappeared at the end of those words. *Why was he telling Millie all of this?*

"She told me she was speaking for her grandma and that she realized yesterday, when she went on a boat ride with Ace, that she was here because her grandmother had sent her. Now, don't get me wrong, I feel that same way sometimes, and I could see her grandma doing that. It's like we realized that maybe what she said is right. That me and my son can mourn the loss of the one we both loved differently but that we shouldn't not let the other one mourn the way he needed to. And that is my fault.

"I tried to make my son give up his bull riding, give up his business and take his mom's champion pictures off his walls. And when he refused, I loaded up, hired someone to sell my home and I drove away and ended up here. No one knew me. There were lots of fishing holes around, so I opened my store. And now here I stand. My granddaughter basically told me that she's not backing down. She said she knows her grandma sent her here and she's supposed to direct this and get me and her dad back together and that she knows her grandma wants that."

*Wow.* Millie's insides churned. *Oh, how she knew what he was feeling.* When you lost the man or woman you loved, your emotions were crazy, confused—and you couldn't change them until the time of reckoning was right. You could look at both sides with open eyes and you could choose what mattered the most. She didn't have a granddaughter to care about or need to find a way to love her and everyone around her like he was having to do. It was obvious to everyone how much he loved that girl. And same for Kelsy but now, knowing all of the story, Millie was spinning.

"I didn't have to face what you are facing but I can tell you that if I could feel my husband up there telling me to make sure to not let his death mess up my relationship with the people he loved…we didn't have those people. Yes, I had my parents and granddad for a while, but no problems. But to us, it was me and him first. But I'd do it, if that had been my situation. After he was killed, I holed up for a long time and I had no one I had to try to make happy, just myself. And that's what I've been doing. And looking at what you've been doing, I feel bad for you."

Without thinking, she reached out and cupped his bicep with her hand. She felt the strength in that muscle and she squeezed. "You're a strong man. I know that not just because I'm holding your arm and I feel your muscle, but because you have inner strength. You are steadfast, solid in what you believe in and how you love. And that's probably why your wife loved you. And I can see that if you've been living all these years away from your family, that she might be pushing on you a bit."

She gave him a soft smile. "That's what I'd be doing. If I had anyone else to love and my emotions were standing in the way of that, I can tell you my husband would be…" A shaky, emotion-filled laugh escaped. "He would probably be giving me a big ole push like a cow would have done."

She laughed, couldn't help it. Just thinking about it struck her: he could be doing that on other things, like opening her life up to more people. She'd been doing it slowly and was realizing that she'd missed people. Friends. She didn't need to be thinking about that right now. She looked at this man in front of her, standing in real boots and with real pain in his eyes, and she knew that for some reason, he'd been sent to her for her to give him this message.

"I can tell by looking at you that you know what you are supposed to do. And I don't know why we ran into each other but now I feel like I'm supposed to tell you, just like Kelsy did, that it's time to bring your family back together. Make your wife smile. Make her happy." She felt tears in her words and her heart, and she held his gaze.

~*~

Lumas stared at Millie, this strong woman, and he understood this hadn't been a coincidence. She'd said exactly what he'd needed to hear. She pulled her hand away from his arm after giving it one more gentle squeeze, and he just stared at her.

"Thank you. You're right." His words rumbled as he fought off emotion. "We've been through similar heartbreaks, and I believe you've given me the right message. I just needed one more person to kick me in the rear and help me get to my business. *So,* I'm heading to my son's house and I'm going to make things right. I'm going to make my granddaughter happy. And my wife. And I just need to tell you thank you. Maybe I needed that kick in the rear but you did it in a gentle way, a heartfelt way of understanding."

His heart tightened as the corners of her lips lifted and her eyes softened with understanding. He knew the feeling was from the emotions he was going through—that was all it was, but he really appreciated her.

He turned and headed back toward his truck, then

stopped and turned back toward her. "But, wait—I need to help you finish this."

She laughed. "No, you don't need to do that. I am a strong woman. Believe me." She held up her arm and squeezed her bicep tight so that it popped to attention, like she was a weight lifter. "I can take care of this myself. I'm just glad that I got to help you today. So go on. I'll haul that all over here and then I'll head into work. And good luck."

He smiled. They stared at each other for a minute, and then he turned and got in his truck and headed back to his house. He could get there before Kelsy headed to the store. He'd pack a bag and he'd head out. And if she wanted to go with him, she could. He felt like this needed to be between him and his son, her dad, but he'd give her a choice. That was what he would be doing from here on out. He wouldn't be choosing for someone; he'd let them choose what was right for them in rough situations, not what he chose for them. He was done with that. It was a new day. As he drove, he knew his sweet, strong wife was smiling.

# CHAPTER FOURTEEN

It was the third week since she had moved here to spend time with her granddad, to get to know him better, and her life had changed. Her granddad had come home that Saturday before she headed to work, and he'd told her that after talking to her, he had run into Millie Watts. The wonderful Millie who had understood what he was going through, and he had opened up to her. And that amazing woman had understood. And after talking to her, Granddad was going to make up with her dad, his son. She'd instantly wanted to go, and her granddad had told her she could. He'd given her the choice but then she'd realized that this wasn't her choice. This was between her granddad and her dad. And she needed to stay out of it.

She needed to stay here in town and wait. And she

had. Her granddad had driven all the way to the bull ranch outside of Dallas, and from what he told her when he'd come home two days later with a big smile on his face, they had both been worked on. She had worked on him, and her mom had worked on her dad. She'd been just as determined to have her family back together as Kelsy and her grandmother. And they'd all made up.

She'd thanked her mom for helping them work through their issues, and now they would all be so happy. The men they loved had now accepted their loss of the lady they both loved—well, they loved her and her mom too, but they'd come to peace with what had happened.

Granddad had actually gone into her dad's office and looked at all those wonderful pictures of her talented grandmother, his bride smiling and happy. Living life like she loved it and had worked so hard to be able to do so well. And Granddad had known, he told her when he got home, that seeing that smile again like that had reminded him that she had been doing what she loved, and he couldn't take that away from her. No matter how hard he'd tried. And when he accepted that, he'd known that she had felt peace, wonderful peace.

Today, she had another mission. She had been at the diner eating with Genna and that sweet helper, Jasmine. Caleb Buckley had come in, and he had paused at their table. She'd noticed that his gaze lingered on Jasmine, but not for long, as he said hello to all of them and then focused on Kelsy.

"I tell you, the beaver dam is coming along, and Ace is thrilled about it."

She hadn't seen Ace Buckley since their ride to the beaver area. "Really? It was so great seeing what they'd started and that it's not going to hurt that gorgeous lake that is already there."

"That's what he said, too. Listen, if you ever want to go out there and look at it, feel free to do so."

His words were a bit odd to her. "Maybe I could take my granddad one day."

He nodded. "That place is great, and you have permission to go if you want. Ace is out there today, helping the beavers get settled in. Don't ask me what he's doing, because I really don't know. But I know y'all discovered them together, so it's just as much your right to go out there and see what's going on, if you're interested." He smiled at her, tipped his hat, and headed to a back table where some cowboys sat.

She watched him go, wondering what in the world he'd meant by all of that. She wasn't going out there to interrupt Ace. He hadn't asked her to come out there. Then she'd turned and settled back into her booth seat and saw that both Genna and Jasmine stared at her as if she were dumb. "Okay, so why are y'all looking at me like that?"

Genna tapped her finger on the table. "Well, the entire family has noticed that something is wrong with Ace. He's quieter than usual, sticking to himself, and he's been taking a lot of trips to the lake out there where he and his dad used to hang out. The place where you and him went. Now we're all wondering, everyone is curious and wondering if you have any idea what's going on?"

She really didn't. She knew that she wished she could see him but she wasn't going to push him. Now that she was getting her family back together, she wished she could thank him. Her mom and dad were coming to the next dance, which was next Saturday. They were going to come stay with her and her granddad. It was going to be the first family gathering since she was eight years old. Tears built in the back of her eyes and she fought them off. Just the thought of how he'd helped her did that to her.

It suddenly dawned on her that she'd been so caught up in worrying about her family, she hadn't let herself even think about how Ace was doing, or whether something was wrong. No, she hadn't seen him. She'd been working at the store while her granddad was gone, and he hadn't been in. And even now that Granddad was back, he still hadn't been in. Was he avoiding her? Now she sat there with Genna and Jasmine staring at her as if she were missing something—*was she?*

"I think I better go out there and check on him. Is that what y'all are thinking?"

They hooked their heads to the side and hitched their brows, as if saying, *boy, she really is dumb*…then they nodded in agreement.

*What was going on?*

Yes, she knew she could fall for the amazing

cowboy. Oh yeah, she knew it. She'd known the night he'd danced with her. But that night, during their only dance, he'd made it totally clear that he had no interest in relationships. And that day he'd brought her home from the trip down the stream, and the moments on the pier after he'd held her so gently and helped her…kissed her. During their beaver adventure, her eyes had opened to how she was meant to help her dad and granddad, he'd been cold and drawn in. That was the last time she'd seen him.

She'd had plenty to deal with but now she realized that he, no matter what, had helped her deal with this, one of the most important things in her life, her family getting reunited. And she hadn't thanked him—which she needed to do. Had to do.

She'd thanked him for his words and his comfort that day on the pier but since then, she hadn't thanked him for everything good that had come out of their day.

She reached for her purse, now suddenly in a hurry. She pulled out a twenty dollar bill and laid it on the table, knew there was enough there to pay for her sandwich and glass of water. She looked at the ladies, who now sat straight and watched her with big smiles. She suddenly knew she had to go out there.

This was *extremely* important.

"I'll see you two later." And then she left them. She knew as she walked out the door that they were probably doing high fives, slapping their palms together because they were so happy she was heading out to confront Ace. Because that was exactly what she was going to do.

As she made it to her car, Josie Jane came from behind her and called her name. She turned back; Ruby was with her as the two hustled toward her. They were grinning.

"So you sure do act like you're in a hurry," Josie Jane said.

Ruby chuckled. "Got somewhere to go that you're late for?"

"Yes, why?" That was all she could get out.

Ruby handed her a paper bag. "There's a big piece of cake in there and a couple of forks, in case you get out there in the boonies and y'all need a treat. Oh, I'm not supposed to know where you're going but I overheard your conversation with the ladies. So I made sure there was enough cake in there for you to share with the young man who might be hungry."

She grinned. *Oh goodness.* "Thank you. Now, I'll see you ladies later."

Josie Jane smiled, her eyes dancing. "Your granddad is fine. And he's very excited about your mom and dad coming. We're all very happy that we're going to get to meet them. And we know that Millie kind of helped him with that, and we're pleased about that too. We love our Millie, and I think she's glad she was able to help."

"I love Millie too," Kelsy said, and it was true. "I hope she's doing good."

"I think she might actually be over at your granddad's store. At least that's where I thought I saw her heading right after she closed up for the day. You three were eating a very early dinner today."

It was true; she'd gone to meet with Jasmine and Genna as soon as they'd called her and ordered the sandwich because the chicken salad was too good to pass up. Now her curiosity was revved up. *Had she been set up with all of this? The lunch that opened her eyes to the fact that she and Ace needed to have a talk? Caleb coming in and mentioning Ace? And leaving her granddad alone so that he might have a visitor too?* Surely not, but it was suddenly a possibility. "So she went to Granddad's fishing store? She doesn't fish."

Josie Jane grinned. "She went, and that's a first. Maybe something is brewing over there, like a new fisherwoman."

She glanced at where Millie's store was. From where she stood, her granddad's store wasn't visible but she knew that Millie had a clear view of her granddad's place. A clear view of who came, who went, and when he was there by himself. She suddenly wondered if maybe, just maybe that's what she'd been waiting on: the chance for him to be alone. Kelsy wasn't going to push it, but she hoped something might come of this. But right now she had something else to deal with. She had to go find Ace.

She turned and put the bag of cake inside, then slid into her seat. She waved and then headed down the road. It was a fairly long drive, and she wished it wasn't. But she also hoped she could remember exactly how to get there and find the man she just…needed to talk to. Just needed to see.

~*~

Ace had been watching the beavers more than he needed to, but he'd been here anyway, watching from a distance as they cut their trees down, and watched the land behind their new home fill with water. There was now on this land a small pond, a stream, and a lake with lots of wonderful memories. He was glad; he had memories, recent memories that took place here, and he wasn't dealing with them well.

Often—no, not often—but every time he was here, he had Kelsy on his mind. Couldn't put away the memory of kissing sweet, beautiful inside and out, and hopefully now, very happy Kelsy. He'd been told that her mom and dad were coming for a visit. He hadn't gone into the store but her granddad had called him and told him. As if Lumas had known why he wasn't coming by the store, so he had made sure Ace knew what was going on. Ace had a strange feeling that people in town had a notion that something was going on between him and Kelsy. They didn't know that he wasn't going to allow anything to actually go on. He couldn't help but wonder why they got that thought when he was keeping his mouth closed and his distance. But he was so happy Kelsy had reunited her family and grateful that he'd been able to help her. Still, he was avoiding her.

He had pulled away on purpose and knew that he couldn't…yeah, he knew he could have feelings for her and he couldn't do it. Couldn't admit to it or humor those feelings. But here, here in this beautiful spot, he could think about his dad and his mom like he always had. The people he missed, the people who had left him and his brother. The people he loved. His life goal was to never do as they had done—leave those he loved behind. Yeah, he wasn't a child anymore, but he couldn't take that chance. He knew how hard it was if you really loved someone to know that you weren't in control of your life and you didn't control when you come into life or when you leave. And in doing that, he just didn't want to be the one who ever left his child or wife behind.

His heart clenched as he sat there in his canoe among the new grassy lake, the lake that had lots of trees inside, surrounded by the foot-high water. Where he sat, he could also see through the trees to the main lake because many had been cut down by the beavers, giving him two views to take in from his canoe. And as he sat there with Kelsy on his mind, she appeared through the trees, standing on the stone pier.

He was seeing things, he figured. She had walked to the end and she stood there with her hands on her jean-clad hips. Her hair shone in the late afternoon sun, and he realized she wasn't a hallucination. It was a Saturday afternoon and she'd probably left and given her granddad time with his fans. *But why was she here?*

Then, as if sensing his eyes were on her, she turned and peered through the lack of trees, that did still give him some coverage. But then she lifted her hand and waved. His heart rumbled; it tumbled, and then it rolled off the cliff, dove to his feet, bounced out of the canoe, and hit the water. He was a goner and he knew it. He'd been denying it and he kept trying. But sitting there, looking at her…oh how badly he wanted to go and pull her into his arms. Like that day they'd stood on that pier and he'd known in his heart of hearts that he was in trouble, especially after she kissed him.

Then, as he watched, she cupped her hands around her mouth and called his name. He didn't move; he'd frozen up, and then she walked off the pier and started to walk down the grassy edge of the lake toward him as she continued to call his name. He just sat there. Then the beavers heard her; it was afternoon and they'd started to move about. Now they started to chatter; then the frogs, the many frogs that had taken up among the wet weeds and trees in the wetlands, started to burp and grunt and make all kinds of noise. Then the birds that had taken up residence in the trees, enjoying the coolness of the swampy lands, started to sing. And he sat there in his canoe, dumbfounded.

She stopped calling his name as she reached the edge where the water was still low, knee-deep, which was the depth he and the canoe were sitting in. It was deeper out where the beavers were building but this was the lowland. His feet weren't getting wet or running toward her like they wanted to do. His brain told him he had to move, but what did he do? He sat there.

He wanted to go over there and sweep her into his arms and kiss her pretty mouth and tell her he loved her. That was not what he'd ever wanted to do before and he knew if he did, he'd pay a price. He'd have to worry for the rest of his life if they were going to have children and if he'd leave them behind.

"I love you!" he heard her shout. And then he heard it again: "I *love* you!" Her voice wavered.

Tears filled his eyes, and he watched as she stepped into the water and walked in the knee-deep water, through the bushes and the submerged grass and vines. He started to move, turning his canoe in her direction. He paddled fast, zooming past trees and bushes, determined to get her out of that water that could hold dangers.

She didn't stop. They met halfway, her in the water and him in the canoe. His heart thundered; her face was bright with a red blush and a smile bright below tears rolling down her face.

"What are you doing?" he managed to ask.

"I came to tell you thank you for what you did for my granddad, my dad and my mom. But when I got here, when I saw you all the way out here among this beautiful wonder of nature, this sanctuary you're letting the beavers create and enjoy and for you to hide in…I knew that I couldn't deny it any longer. The words I'm saying are true and for you. Ace, I love you. And if you marry me, if you told me you loved me and we got married and I had only one day with you, or fifty years with you or more, I would be grateful for every second I got to be called your wife. For every moment that you held me and told me you loved me. I would never regret it. I would be thankful for the gift. You may think I'm crazy," she said through her tear-filled voice. "You may tell me to go away, but I had to tell you. But, if you don't feel any of that, I'll turn and I'll make my way back through this beautiful, beautiful sanctuary that you've let happen, and I won't say it again. I'll leave you alone."

She stared at him, her beautiful eyes glistening in the sun that peeked through the trees around them. *He could let her go.*

Save her any anguish she might ever feel. But,

could he survive watching her walk away?

Survive the anguish of letting the best thing that had ever happened to him walk out of his life?

In that moment, he knew the answer. He rolled out of the canoe, went into the water, and then he jumped up, soaked and smiling and ready to live life to the fullest. He took her into his arms and held her close as he kissed her temple.

"I love you," he said, and she looked up at him. "You're making my dreams come true. I love you. I love you. I. Love. You." He smiled down at her. "I'll always cherish that and like you said, I can't turn away. I thought I could. I'm out here hiding, just like you said. This is my hiding spot, but Kelsy, I don't want it to be my hiding spot anymore I want it to be *our* spot. Our place of peace and happiness. Our place where love found us. Thank you for not giving up on me."

She smiled and then she slipped her hand around his neck and, like she'd done before, she tugged his lips to hers. But this time, he pulled her tight. Standing there in the water, with the birds singing, the beavers chattering, and the frogs singing bass, he kissed her with everything in him.

# EPILOGUE

"So, everybody, we're having a dance," Lumas said, from the microphone, as all the people on the dance floor stood and looked up at the grinning man.

Kelsy stood there in front of her grandfather, holding the hands of the man she'd just married. Her sweet, wonderful Ace.

Her mom and dad stood to the side; they were so happy. They'd come here and loved it. She'd never seen two adult men so content in all of her life—her dad and her granddad—and when they learned she and Ace were getting married, they'd jumped in wholeheartedly. And this dance tonight, she had decided—and her husband went along—would be their wedding night and their second dance together.

Everyone had been excited. Josie Jane, Ruby,

Genna, Jasmine…and Millie. Oh, sweet Millie. She was beautiful tonight, and Kelsy thought with all of her heart that Millie looked at her granddad with something that was more than just friendship. And Kelsy hoped, prayed that she was right.

But right now, as her granddad stood there grinning at her and his buddy Ace—now his grandson-in-law— he smiled and continued. "Tonight, there's a dance that we've had requested by the bride and groom on this amazing night. This town has created a wonderful gathering for love…sometimes to find its way and sometimes just wonderful dances. And for the first time in a very long time, I may dance tonight." His gaze went over to where Millie stood.

Oh, Kelsy hoped that was going to happen.

Then he looked back at her and Ace. "These two newlyweds are going to have the first dance. But we're not having just any dance. We're going to let these two dance to their now favorite song, good ole Brad Paisley singing 'Long Sermon.' And so I hope you can all be happy watching this now loving, wonderful couple who helped bring our family back together and make Lone

Star not just my home but now my family's happy place. A great place to gather and enjoy life together. So this dance is for you two. Then, we're all going to dance and have a wonderful time tonight, and as far as I'm concerned, these dances will continue."

And then the song began.

Ace grinned at her. "Well, darlin', are you ready?"

She smiled up at him. Her heart thundered in her chest, at the feel of his arm around her and her hand in his, and those eyes looking into hers. "I'm ready always. Now, let's do this. Show me what you've got, cowboy, because I know your sweet mom taught you well. And I can't wait to dance with the likes of you one more time and forevermore."

Then he led the way, and she happily joined in.

# More Books by Hope Moore

**Billionaire Cowboys of Lone Star, Texas**

Forever Love'n Cowboy

Sweet Love'n Cowboy

Heart Love'n Cowboy

Love Catch'n Cowboy

**McCoy Billionaire Brothers**

Her Billionaire Cowboy's Fake Marriage

Her Billionaire Cowboy's Fake Wedding Fiasco

Her Billionaire Cowboy's Trouble in Paradise

Her Billionaire Cowboy's Secret Baby Surprise

Her Billionaire Cowboy's Second Chance Romance

Her Billionaire Cowboy Fake Fiancé

Her Billionaire Cowboy's Inconvenient Marriage Blessing

**Billionaire Cowboys of True Love, Texas**

Billionaire Cowboy's Runaway Bride

Billionaire Cowboy's Wedding Crasher

Her Billionaire Cowboy's Hill Country Proposal

Billionaire Cowboy Auctioned at Christmas

Billionaire Cowboy's Dream Come True

# About the Author

Hope Moore is the pen name of an award-winning author who lives deep in the heart of Texas surrounded by Christian cowboys who give her inspiration for all of her inspirational sweet romances. She loves writing clean & wholesome, swoon worthy romances for all of her fans to enjoy and share with everyone. Her heartwarming, feel good romances are full of humor and heart, and gorgeous cowboys and heroes to love. And the spunky women they fall in love with and live happily-ever-after.

When she isn't writing, she's trying very hard not to cook, since she could live on peanut butter sandwiches, shredded wheat, coffee...and cheesecake why should she cook? She loves writing though and creating new stories is her passion. Though she does love shoes, she's admitted she has an addiction and tries really hard to stay out of shoe stores. She, however, is not addicted to social media and chooses to write instead of surf FB - but she LOVES her readers so she's working on a free novella just for you and if you sign up for her newsletter she will send it to you as soon as its ready! You'll also receive snippets of her adventures, along with special deals, sneak peaks of soon-to-be released books and of course any sales she might be having.

She promises she will not spam you, she hates to be spammed also, so she wouldn't dare do that to people she's crazy about (that means YOU). You can unsubscribe at any time.

Sign up for my newsletter at:
www.subscribepage.com/hopemooresignup

I can't wait to hear from you.

*Hope Moore~*
Always hoping for more love, laughter and reading for you every day of your life!

www.ingramcontent.com/pod-product-compliance
Lightning Source LLC
Chambersburg PA
CBHW070645100726
47907CB00007B/2104